I guess also, deep down, I wasn't sure they would necessarily like our costumes or the cheers, but I felt it was too late to back out now. I didn't know about other guys from our class coming, hoping we'd be terrible. I'd figured it would be just girls. What if the guys boo when we come out? But I don't think they'd do that, since it's our school. They've got to have some school spirit....

"NORMA KLEIN has a nice sense of what teenagers today might be feeling about themselves, each other, their bodies and minds, their friends and parents."

The New York Times

"NORMA KLEIN has a great knack for creating characters of warmth and likability. She is sharp and perceptive, but kind. She knows what makes people tick...."

The Boston Globe

Fawcett Juniper Books
by Norma Klein:

ANGEL FACE

BEGINNERS' LOVE

BIZOU

IT'S OKAY IF YOU DON'T LOVE ME

LOVE IS ONE OF THE CHOICES

THE QUEEN OF THE WHAT IFS

SNAPSHOTS

GIVE AND TAKE

THE CHEERLEADER

Norma Klein

FAWCETT JUNIPER • NEW YORK

RLI: $\frac{\text{VL Grades 5 + up}}{\text{IL Grades 6 + up}}$

A Fawcett Juniper Book
Published by Ballantine Books

Library of Congress Catalog Card Number: 85-224

ISBN 0-449-70190-5

This edition published by arrangement with Alfred A. Knopf, Inc.

Manufactured in the United States of America

First Ballantine Books Edition: November 1986

For Natalie Babbit

1

NOW THAT I'M IN EIGHTH GRADE MY SCHOOL lets us go out for lunch. Usually my best friend, Karim, and I go to the pizza place around the corner or the Bagel Shop down the block. It partly depends on whether we feel like eating with a crowd of other kids or just talking by ourselves. Even though I'm glad I go to a coed school, you don't always feel like having girls around. The pizza place is so crowded, there's no way you can have a conversation about anything.

At the Bagel Shop we took our orders to a table in the back. Karim pulled some tickets out of his pocket. "I got them," he said, sort of shyly.

I took the tickets and looked at them. Four first-row seats to the Go-Go's concert at Radio City! "Fantastic!" I said. "How'd your father get them?"

"He knows someone," Karim said.

It seems like Karim's father always knows someone. He's gotten us tickets to a Knicks game, to a McEnroe-Connors final, and even to a Michael Jackson concert. He's an Arab, but last year he moved his family, which consists of him, Karim and Karim's mother, Susie, who's American, to New York City. He says you get better value for your money here. They live in the Parker Meridien hotel because Karim's parents travel a lot and his mother isn't that big on houskeeping. To me it's a great setup. Not only is his mother not around most of the time to scream at him about cleaning up his room, there's even a maid service. If Karim goes out for a hamburger or something at night, they remake the bed while he's away, and sometimes even turn down the sheets and leave him some chocolates with a card saying SLEEP WELL. You have to be pretty amazingly rich to live like that day in and day out. My stepfather, Harold, says a day's rent at the Meridien is probably more than he earns in a month.

"So, who do you want to go with?" I asked.

Karim looked around the Bagel Shop to make sure no one was there from our class. "Rachel."

"She's your first choice?"

"She's my only choice," Karim said.

Karim just entered the Haines School last year, so he hasn't known Rachel Ecker as long as I have. He didn't even have girls in his classes at the school he used to go to, so he's not really used to them yet. I've been at Haines since kindergarten, and I can remember all the mean things Rachel's been doing since she was five years old: making fun of people, dumping sand on top of my painting while it was still wet, doing imitations of new kids and giggling hysterically when they came into the room. But in the last year or so Rachel has, even I have to admit, gotten outstandingly attractive. She has shiny black hair and blue eyes and the beginning of what could be what Harold calls an A-plus supercalifragilisticexpialidocious figure. To me that doesn't make up for her character, but I can see how if you hadn't known her that long, it might.

"What if she doesn't want to go?" I said. "Don't you have another choice?"

He shook his head mournfully.

"Okay," I said, finishing my Coke. "I'll see what I can do."

"Do you think she'll say yes?" he asked eagerly.

"Sure," I said. I didn't want to add that Rachel might say yes just because she wanted to go to the concert, not because she especially likes Karim. I don't know if it's because he's a foreigner or what, but Karim is actually scared of girls. He says he thinks about them a lot, but he never knows what to say to them. I don't have that problem at all. Sure, it's easier to talk to boys, but so it's a girl? I don't see what there is to be scared about. Some girls are weird, some are nice—that's just the way God or whoever set it up.

Actually lots of boys in our class are just like Karim. They'll get a crush on some girl, but they don't have the courage to ask her out. That's where I come in. I'll call the girl up for whoever it is and kind of ask around to see if she's interested. If she is, I'll report back and then he'll call her. Mom says I should run a computer dating service. The way I figure it is: Why not help people if they've got a particular problem? Since sixth grade I've had various girlfriends, but the one I like best is still Laurie, because she has the good points of a boy—she says what she really thinks and doesn't flirt around—combined with some of the good points of a girl, in that she's friendly and interested in other people. For instance, when I broke my leg skiing last year, she'd call me up every day and read me the homework on the phone and tell me everything that'd happened in school. It was almost like I didn't miss anything.

I figured I'd call Rachel after dinner. That's the Prime Time to call girls, in case you want any tips about it. If you call them right after school, they're usually out at dancing lessons or they have some friend over. But right after dinner they're probably just watching TV and they're in a more mellow mood.

Rachel answered the phone when I called. "Hi, Rachel, it's Evan."

"Hi, Evan." She sounded surprisingly friendly. "What's up?"

"Well, nothing special. . . . I just wondered if maybe you might be interested in going to the Go-Go's concert in two weeks."

"The Go-Go's! Wow! Do you have tickets?"

"Yeah."

"God, how amazing. . . . Sure, I'd love to. That's really nice of you to think of me. Would it just be the two of us?"

I cleared my throat. Here's where the diplomatic part of it comes in. "No, well, actually, the thing is, they're

Karim's tickets. He wanted you to come as his date. I'll be going with Laurie."

"So, why didn't he call me himself?'

"He's sort of shy. And he knows I've known you a longer time."

There was a pause. "Why can't it be the *other* way—he can go with Laurie and I'll go with you?"

I didn't want to say because I didn't want her as my date and wouldn't even if it were my last chance on earth to go to a rock concert, or anywhere else. "They're his tickets, and he likes you."

"So either I go as his date or I don't go?"

"Right."

Another long pause and then a sigh. "Okay. Well, why not? . . . He really likes me? As a girlfriend?"

"Yeah." Don't ask me why, but he does. "Do *you* like *him*?"

Rachel laughed. "Come *on*, Evan! He's so weird! The way he dresses, everything. The way he talks. 'I was at such a lovely restaurant last night.'" She mimicked the slight English accent Karim has. "He doesn't even live in an apartment, someone said. He lives in a hotel!"

"I know," I said, really getting pissed off. "I've been there. He's my best friend!"

"I don't see why," she said. "You're so normal. . . . How come you're friends?"

"I like him," I said. "How come Daphne Caldwell is *your* best friend? She has so many bubbles in her head, you couldn't pump them out with a bicycle pump."

"That's not true!" Rachel said indignantly. "Daphne just spends a lot of time studying ballet, so she doesn't do so well in school. Okay, well, like I said, I'll go only because it's not going to be a real date. I mean, make sure he realizes that I'm not going to—"

"But will you act nice?" I said. "Will you at least talk to him in a friendly way?"

"Sure," Rachel said. "I'm great at that. Have no fear."

After I hung up, I felt depressed. Why did Karim have to get a crush on Rachel? It's true there aren't millions of great girls in our class, but in personality she's the pits, in my opinion. Like she's doing him this big favor just by going, when lots of girls would be really excited and pleased.

I called Karim back and told him it was all set. "She said yes?" he said.

"Yeah, she was really excited."

"You're an excellent friend, Evan," he said. "I could never have done that myself."

"Yeah, well, it ought to be fun," I said. We talked some more and then I hung up.

For a couple of minutes I just sat in the hall staring into space, feeling like a jerk. Harold, my stepfather, walked by, carrying a sheaf of his drawings. He's an illustrator and he works at home, mostly. "Did the world end today or yesterday?" he said, seeing my expression.

I told him the situation. "Listen, Evan, if you're that guy's best friend, have a talk with him. Tell him girls like that are murder. She'll eat him alive. He's just a kid."

"She doesn't like him enough to eat him alive," I said gloomily.

Harold laughed. "You've got a point. They save their

reall ammunition for the ones they like. Boy, why didn't I know you when I was in junior high? I just sat and dreamed my way through till college, practically. But, no, I was too weird. It wouldn't have worked."

"Yeah, I can imagine," I said, grinning.

He bopped me on the head in a playful way. "Thanks, kid."

Frankly, Harold is still weird, but I like him. Actually, I hate to say this, but I like him more than I like my real father. Maybe it's that my parents split when I was four and my real father moved to Florida, so I've never seen him that much. When I was eight, Mom met Harold, who'd been married before but who never had kids. My older brother, Gary, was eleven then. Harold says he's glad. He says he breaks into hives at the sight of a baby and thinks kids should be taken away from their parents at birth and brought back when they can tell dirty jokes and are toilet-trained. "Here, I got two ready-made sons with neuroses I'm not even responsible for! Plus a sexy, smart lady with a great net game at tennis. What more can a man ask for?"

When I say weird about Harold, I mean *weird*. For instance, he's the only person I've met, other than me, who went through a whole year of his life eating meals backward, starting with the dessert and ending with the main course. The reason I stopped doing that was I realized it did take my appetite away for the main course. I'd been trying to prove to Mom that there wasn't any connection. But Harold said he just stopped because it was too much trouble. It *never* took his appetite away!

And sometimes now he'll have a slice of peach pie or some chocolate pudding right before we have dinner. When Mom married him, she said it was like adopting another kid.

AT SCHOOL THE NEXT DAY KARIM KEPT GAZ-ing longingly at Rachel. I knew she'd already told her friends, because they were giggling and staring at him. One thing she said *is* true about Karim—he dresses strangely. His mother is a fashion designer and she gets him things like silk shirts and handmade cowboy boots with jewels on them. Everything looks too new, probably because once he's worn something a few times, she gives it away. She mostly designs clothes for women, but lately she's been doing stuff for men and boys, and she likes to try them on him first. What I mean is, he doesn't look bad, but he doesn't fit in with everyone else either.

Laurie took me aside at lunch hour. "Does it have to be Rachel?" she said. "She's such a snob."

"He likes her," I explained, shrugging.

"Well, he's sure got rotten taste," Laurie said. "Tell him there's more to life than boobs and a nose job."

"I tried. . . . But we'll have fun, anyway. We can just ignore her."

I think Laurie's a little sensitive on the subject of women's figures because she hasn't got much of anything yet. I still think she's sexy, but it's more her personality.

At the end of study hour, Marlon Rodowsky was talking about some ice-hockey game he was going to.

"Boy, how'd you get tickets?" someone asked.

"My father knows somebody," he said.

My father knows nobody and he still lives in Florida, and Harold doesn't even know ice hockey *exists*. "We're going to the Go-Go's," I said.

Marlon looked contemptuous. "What's that—some kind of girls' group?"

"So?" I said. "They're Number Seven on the Top Forty."

"It'd be different if it was X or Duran Duran," Willy Duncan said.

"The Go-Go's are better," Karim put in. "I've seen those other groups, and they don't compare."

Everyone looked at him.

"Where'd you see them?" Marlon asked.

"I saw Duran Duran in London last summer," Karim said, "and X at a private club."

"Pardon me for living," Willy said.

Karim turned red. He walked out of the room.

"Listen, he can't help it if he's rich," I said. "Leave him alone."

"He's always boasting about it, that's all," Willy said.

"It's *not* boasting. He was just answering your question."

"Rachel's only going with him because she wants to go to the concert," Marlon said. "She told me she wouldn't make out with him if he was the last guy on earth."

That's so typical of Rachel. She can't keep her mouth shut for one second! "Well, probably if he'd been in this country longer, he'd have better taste in girls," I said.

But Marlon was staring at Rachel, who was practicing a cheerleading step in the corner of the room with some of her friends.

The only sport I'm really into is swimming. The reason I swim is, I had a heart operation when I was a really little kid and even though I'm fine now, the doctor said it would be best to take it easy. I'm glad, in a way. I agreed with Harold. When someone asks what sport he's good at, he says, "Watching." He says being a good spectator is a lost art. He also claims people who aren't that good at sports are better at watching, because they're playing the game in their head. Actually, there is one part of baseball I like almost as much as watching real games—it's being an umpire. I have a really good eye, and I make excellent calls. You probably don't realize how much skill is involved in umpiring, but, believe me, you have to be really quick, because if you give a wrong call, someone's going to want to kill you. That happens sometimes even if you give a right call. There've been times I wasn't absolutely sure of a call, but you have to stick by what you say the first time or *everyone* ends up hating you.

Marlon is the best pitcher on the team. He was

watching Rachel do her routine. Laurie hates that. She says cheerleaders are fools and grovel before boys and she wouldn't be one in a thousand years. I haven't given it a lot of thought. It's true some cheerleaders are fools, like Rachel, but I figure they were that way from birth on, not as a result of cheerleadering.

"Movements like liquid music," Willy said. He's supposedly a poet, but if you ask me, half of his remarks don't even make sense.

"If she was an animal, she'd be a white stallion with her mane blowing in the breeze," Marlon said.

I looked at him. "A stallion? They're males." What a jerk.

"A unicorn," Willy said, sighing. "They're more rare."

Personally I think Rachel would be a llama. She always has that snooty expression llamas have. Marlon and Willy were still staring in a trance while she did her stuff.

After school I went over to Karim's place to hear his new album. His father just gets these albums free, practically before they come out. Some of them are even autographed or come with photos of the stars attached to them with comments like, "Karim, much love, Linda." Karim says it doesn't mean anything—they just know his father, not him. Still, some of those photos or albums might be worth a fortune. Only to Karim that wouldn't mean anything, because he has so much money to begin with.

When we first got to be friends, I couldn't imagine what that would be like. What if you could buy anything in the world you ever wanted and you knew the money would never run out? You'd think if anything would make someone really happy, it would be that. But the trouble is, Karim doesn't know what it's like to live any other way, and till he came to New York, most of the kids he knew were as rich as he is. The only reason he's at the Haines School is his mother went there and she wanted him to meet normal kids, like me. But in a way I think that makes it harder for him, because to us everything he does is a little strange.

"Where's your mom?" I asked.

"In Paris," he said. "They had to go to an opening there."

"What of?"

"One of her friends started designing hats," he said. "They said I could go with them, but then I would've missed school."

That's what I mean. You take a kid like me and ask him if he'd mind missing two days of school to go to Paris and he'd start packing in one second. But to Karim it was no big deal, the Eiffel Tower. He'd rather sit in social studies and have Ms. Boorstein rumble on about the Monroe Doctrine.

Karim's room is the greatest. At home I have to share a room with my brother. It's true it's a big room, but still there's no privacy at all. And, which makes it even less fair, Mom gave Gary this extra room in the back to study in or, as she tactfully put it, "to retreat to if Evan starts coming out of your ears." What if he starts coming out of *my* ears? Where do *I* go? Anyway, Karim happens to be an only child, though I gather his father was married a couple of times before and he has a bunch of half brothers and sisters who're out of college already. Before, his father manly married Arab women, but I guess after a while he decided he wanted someone more modern. Over there, all you have to do to get divorced, if you're a man, is clap your hands and say "New wife!" I admit I just read that somewhere and it may only apply if you're a king or someone high up. Being rich may not be enough.

In Karim's room, *everything* is built-in. You press a button, and the bed comes out of the wall! You press another button, and a stereo slides out! It's almost like being in the control room of the starship *Enterprise*. Everything is at your beck and call. It's too bad I don't come from a country where there are oil wells lying around, or maybe one day I could live like this too. Maybe I'll move to Texas.

"Kar, I was thinking," I said, "maybe for the concert you ought to just, well, wear something more like what I wear. I could lend you something if you want." It sounds absurd for someone like me to lend clothes to someone like Karim, but Rachel had mentioned how he never looks the way a kid of our age should.

"Would you?" Karim said. "That would be great. My mother won't be here that weekend so she won't be able to check up on me."

I guess his mother gets hurt if he refuses to wear the stuff she designs. I'm lucky that way. My mom's a social worker and she only notices if something I wear is what she calls "filthy beyond recall." "It's lucky we're the same size," I said.

Karim sighed. "Sometimes I get the feeling Rachel really likes Marlon."

"He's a jerk," I said.

"Yeah, but he's good at sports. You said yourself—he's the best pitcher Haines has ever had."

"Sports aren't everything." I said that to make him feel better, but the thing is, if there's no sport you're good at, it's true it does lower your image with guys *and* girls. Karim didn't grow up playing most of the sports we do, but also, he's just really uncoordinated. He just kind of stands there. Maybe he's not aggressive enough or something.

"I think, in America, sports are very, *very* important," Karim said. "And I will never be good. Even your girlfriend, Laurie, is excellent."

Laurie's the star of the girls' softball team. She's little, but very fast on her feet. "Yeah, well, Rachel's not so hot at sports."

"But she can cheerlead," Karim said.

"That's not a sport," I pointed out.

"Why not?" he said. "It takes the same energy and control. Why isn't it a sport?"

"It's just not." A lot of times, with Karim, I find myself trying to explain something that I've just always taken for granted. It's not his fault, he just doesn't have the same points of reference most kids our age do.

AT DINNER THAT NIGHT I ASKED MOM IF IT was okay if I lent Karim some of my clothes for the concert. She said sure.

"What concert is that?" Gary asked.

"The Go-Go's."

"Are you still in that phase?" he said. "Incredible."

My brother is okay a good deal of the time, but he's a real asshole the rest. Like because *he's* been taking bassoon lessons for ten years, he only likes classical music. Every year we have to trek up to the Silvano School and listen to some horrible twelve-hour concert in which he plays a bassoon solo that sounds like a basset hound being sawed in two. Then we go to a party where his teacher, this totally tank-shaped lady named Marguerita, raves on to Mom and Harold about Gary's touch and sensitivity.

"I like rock," Harold said. "Why didn't you get me a ticket?"

"It's Karim's father who got them," I explained. "He knows somebody."

Harold reached for another roll. "All my life I've wanted to know somebody. And all I know is nobodies like myself. Where's the justice in life?"

"What does Karim's father look like?" Mom asked. "Does he wear one of those long white robes like a sheik?"

"No, he just wears regular business suits. Maybe he wears white robes when he goes back home. Oh, Mom, I—"

"My report card's on the desk," Gary put in.

That's so typical of him! He interrupts what I'm saying to say something that has nothing to do with the subject and does have to do with what he's good at—getting fantastic grades. The guy's a real grade-grubber. He never gets under 95 in anything! Personally, I don't think that proves he's so smart. I just think it proves he's a drone and can memorize anything you put in front of him. I don't say that just because my own grades aren't as good; I really think it's true. Harold says I shouldn't worry. He says he didn't learn to read till he was in third grade, and they used to think he was brain-damaged he was so slow. The only thing he was good at was drawing, which is why he became an artist, I guess.

"Yes, I saw it," Mom said. "It's wonderful."

"I didn't do that well in chem," Gary said, pretending to look sad.

"Ninety-two seems pretty good to me," Mom said.

"Well, it would've been 96 if I hadn't screwed up on the final," Gary said.

"If I were you, I'd be terribly proud of your academic record," Mom said. "Wouldn't *you*, sweetie?"

Sweetie means Harold. He said, "If it were me, I'd be in a coma, I'd be so pleased. They'd have to do brain surgery to bring me back to life. . . . What's for dessert?"

"Apple crunch," Mom said.

"Oh, right! I had some just before dinner. It's terrific." Harold sometimes has two desserts, one before dinner and one after. If I tried that, Mom would have my head.

The day of the Go-Go's concern, I brought Karim some clothes. He tried them on and they fit fine. "Do you want to come by my house around six?" I said.

"I thought Boyce might pick everyone up," Karim said.

Boyce is Karim's father's chauffeur. Even when Karim's father is out of town, Boyce has instructions to take Karim anywhere he wants to go in this immense black Rolls-Royce. I had thought we'd just take a cab or get Harold to drop us off, but the idea of arriving in a Rolls seemed kind of cool.

For the concert I wore my black Elton John T-shirt. I put some stuff on my hair so it would stand out in spikes. I wouldn't wear my hair like that in school, but it makes me look a lot older and more interesting. When I went into the living room to wait, Gary rolled his eyes and said, "Gimme a break."

"You look sharp, Ev," Harold said, smiling.

Mom looked like she would've made some negative comment, but decided not to. I once heard her say to my grandmother that it was good for me to "get it out of my system," whatever that means.

"Can I come along?" Harold said.

"It's sold out," I explained.

"No, I mean just for the ride. I've never driven in a Rolls."

My mother just looked at him.

"Darling, you don't realize what these things mean. All my sex fantasies from the age of thirteen on involved expensive foreign cars. It's something women can't understand."

"I guess you could sit in front with Boyce," I said.

"Who's Boyce?" Gary asked.

"He's their chauffeur. He's been with the family since Karim was born."

"God, I love this," Harold said. "It's like *Upstairs, Downstairs*. You'll be upstairs in back, and I'll be downstairs in front. This is going to be one of the high points of my life."

When Karim rang to say they had arrived, Harold and I went down in the elevator together. "Have fun," Mom called, "and you, in the green shirt, come straight home! Remember you're over age for this kind of thing."

Harold looked crestfallen. "Am I?" He turned to me. "I thought I was the perfect age. Thirty-seven. Isn't that the perfect age, Ev?"

"Sure, Harold," I said, to humor him.

Sometimes I wonder why Mom married Harold,

especially when, after she and Dad split up, she said she would never get married again. My real father is serious and quiet and always worried about something. Harold is always talking and telling jokes, but he seems to have a good effect on my mother. She acts a lot happier now than she did when I was a little kid and she and my real father had just gotten divorced.

Harold got in the front with Boyce, and I got in the back with Karim.

"Hi, Harold," Karim said. "I'm sorry I don't have a ticket for you."

"Think nothing of it," Harold said. "Just riding in this car is enough excitement at my advanced age."

First we picked up Laurie. I like the way Laurie looks. In fact, at night sometimes, we look a little alike because her hair's very short and she kind of spikes it out too. But she had on makeup and had put silver stars on her cheeks. When we got to Rachel's building, Karim had to go in and call up for her. I guess she wanted to make a grand entrance.

While we waited in the car, Harold said, "Is this the maiden who turns helpless men into blobs of Silly Putty?"

"You're not kidding," Laurie said, holding my hand. I like the way she just reaches over to hold it when she feels like it.

"I had one of those once," Harold said. "You notice, I'm still not quite right in the head. She used to chain me to her bed and feed me only on canary seeds while she tickled the tips of my toes with a feather."

Boyce was looking at him. He wears a uniform and hat, just like in the movies. "Ah, yes," he said.

"Don't tell me she did it to you, too?" Harold said.

Most people don't know when Harold is serious or joking. In fact, I'm not always sure myself. Boyce laughed.

A minute later Karim and Rachel came out together. She really looked spectacular in a very short skirt, net stockings, and spike heels. I could feel Laurie vibrate with bad feelings. "Hi, Evan, Hi, Laurie. Sorry I'm late." She glanced up front at Harold, who had swiveled around to stare at her. "Who're *you*?"

"A secret admirer," he said.

"He's my stepfather," I said.

"I was a child groom," Harold said. "I'm really much younger than I look. Evan's mother took one look at me playing by the sandbox and decided she had to have me. What could I do? And then I discovered I had two stepsons who were my own age!"

"Don't worry, he's just kidding," I whispered in Rachel's ear.

WE HAD EXCELLENT SEATS FOR THE CONcert—first row, right in the middle. I had Laurie on one side of me and Rachel on the other. I didn't maneuver it that way—it just seemed to work out. The opening group, INXS, isn't one of my favorites, and the lead singer, Mike Hutchence, was nothing special—just a guy in tight pants writhing around, shoving his hips back and forth. But Rachel and Laurie really seemed to like him. They stood up and started dancing in their seats. I wasn't surprised at Rachel doing that. She seems like she'd do just about anything other people are doing, but Laurie! I looked over at Karim. He shrugged. I decided just to sit there and let them make fools of themselves. Then—it was toward the end of his second-to-last number—a girl a few rows behind us ran onstage and started hugging Hutchence. At

Madison Square Garden you couldn't get onstage, but at Radio City it's easier. Eventually some guy in a suit came forward and dragged her off, but not for a couple of minutes.

"Oh, my God," Rachel said, foaming at the mouth. "She got to *touch* him! She *kissed* him! I'm going to do that!" And before we could stop her, she went running up onstage! She flung her arms around Hutchence. He kept playing, but he didn't shake her off. He let her kiss him a million times over and even put his arm around her. I looked over at Karim. He looked miserable. Imagine being one of those rock stars! You just stand there, you don't even sing well, and all these girls go crazy over you. Unbelieveable.

"She's really nuts," I said.

Laurie sighed. "She actually got to *touch* him," she whispered.

I just stared at her. Laurie is usually so smart and cool about everything. Rachel came panting back to our seats, her eyes shining like she'd just seen God. "Oh, I can't believe it," she said. "I did it, I really did it! Oh, my heart's beating so fast, I think I'm going to die!"

"Why did you do it?" Karim asked, puzzled.

"Because he's so—I can't even speak, I'm so excited. He's just so incredibly sexy. I mean, when I touched him, I really felt sparks! And he put his arm around me! He didn't have to do that."

"What do you consider sexy about him?" Karim asked.

Rachel looked at him like he was nuts. "Everything!" she said. "He even *smells* sexy!"

At intermission she and Laurie went off to the ladies'

room. Karim was really looking depressed. "Did he seem that sexy to *you*?" he asked.

"It's just whoever's up there," I said. "If we were up there, girls would come up to us."

"He didn't seem like a very good singer, even."

"He's not. . . . Look, don't worry about it, Kar. Girls just get like that. I guess the music does something to them." But I was already hatching a plan for revenge.

The Go-Go's are fantastic. I mean, there've been girl singers, but none before that do everything, write their own music, play it, *and* sing it. They're all good, but my favorite is Gina, who plays the drums. She never sings, but she plays the drums just as well as a guy. I know because I played the drums in our school orchestra for a couple of years and to be good you have to have everything—rhythm, speed, timing. It's at least as hard as playing the bassoon. About half-way through, when they were getting into "Head Over Heels," I jumped up and grabbed Karim, "Go!" I said.

We ran up the aisle and leaped onto the stage. The Go-Go nearest me was Kathy, who plays bass. I threw my arms around her and gave her a big kiss. She smiled and kept right on playing. Quickly I looked over at Karim. He'd gone over to Charlotte, who was singing as he was kissing her. I have to admit that it was a great feeling—the music coming at you from everywhere, being that close to them. You feel like you're a part of the whole thing. And Rachel was right—there's some kind of electricity that comes off those stars that's more than just sexiness. I would have married any of them right on the spot without thinking twice.

When we came back to our seats, Laurie glared at me. "What's *wrong* with you?" she said.

I grinned. "I got carried away."

"They're in their twenties! They could almost be your mother!"

"Imagine having a mother like that!" I put my arm around her and kissed her.

"I can't *believe* you would actually do a thing like that," Laurie said.

"Just getting even," I whispered.

"But *I* didn't go up there; it was her."

I looked over at Karim and Rachel. Somehow his going up onstage had had the opposite effect my going up had. Rachel was leaning with her head on his shoulder, kissing him. "Laurie, come on," I said. "She's not holding it against *him*. Please."

Laurie softened. "You looked so cute," she said. "I was scared they might keep you and add to their band."

I have to admit that for the rest of the concert, fantasies of the Go-Go's actually adding me to their group kept going through my head. Me and the five of them touring. I'd stay with whichever one of them I liked most at the moment. They'd know everything about sex and would draw straws for the opportunity to teach me new things. It was one of those times when I was really glad nobody can know what you're thinking. If Laurie had, probably she never would have spoken to me again.

Last year, when Laurie and I started going out, we sat down one evening and made two lists. One was things about sex that we weren't sure we'd ever want to do at any age. The other was things we might want to do in a couple of years, when we were sixteen or seventeen. Laurie's first list was a lot longer than mine, and her second list was a lot shorter. My feeling is I'd like to try most things once, at least, and I guess there's more I'd be willing to do even now if anybody felt like doing it with me. But I thought our doing that was good. We ripped up the lists afterward because if Laurie's mother had found them, she might've had a fit. What it did was make me realize what limits there were, as far as Laurie goes, and I can handle that. Girls are more squeamish when it comes to sex, I think. That's just the way they're brought up. According to Harold, most of them don't really get into it till they're thirty. I hope I don't have to wait *that* long.

After the concert Karim asked if we wanted to come back to the Meridien with him. Since it was a Saturday night, we all said yes. Boyce was right in front of the theater in the Rolls, reading the paper. As we walked toward it I heard some girl say, "Look! That must be the Go-Go's car!" Another girl said, "No, it's probably just some millionaire," As I got in I turned around, looked at them, and waved. They'd never know if I was a star or a millionaire or what.

"Who're you waving at?" Laurie wanted to know. She's pretty jealous at times.

"Just some girls," I said, putting my arm around her.

The way it worked out on the way back to the hotel, I sat in back between Laurie and Rachel, and Karim sat in front with Boyce. I felt a little uncomfortable about that, especially because Rachel kind of leaned against me more than was strictly necessary.

"How was the concert?" Boyce asked Karim.

"It was excellent," Karim said.

"Someday I would like to go to a rock concert," Boyce said thoughtfully. "Just to see what it's like."

"You might find it a little loud," Karim said.

He and Boyce really get along. Karim once told me that he's had more conversations about things with Boyce than he has with his father. Partly it's that his father travels so much, but partly it's like me and Harold. I tell Harold things I'd never tell my father, maybe because he isn't my father and also because he's nearer my age.

We went up to Karim's room. He ordered champagne and ginger ale from room service. I don't like champagne that much—I tried to once. Rachel said she loved it, and Laurie said she'd have one glass to see what it was like.

"I love your room!" Rachel said, stretching out on the bed. "It's so beautiful. It's like in a magazine. How do you keep it so neat?"

"The hotel does that," Karim explained. He was sitting next to Rachel, looking at her longingly.

"I guess your mother had the right idea marrying someone with oil wells," Rachel said.

"She married him because she loved him," Karim said stiffly.

"Yeah, if you didn't love someone, what would be the point?" Laurie said. She was sitting next to me on the floor.

Rachel looked taken aback. "My mother says you can't marry just for love. There's a lot more to it than that. You have to be practical, too."

"I don't know," Laurie said. "I want to do it for love. . . . Don't you, Ev?"

"Definitely." I think love includes sex, even though I know the two don't always go together.

When the drinks came, Karim poured champagne for everyone but me, and we toasted by clinking our glasses together. "My father's first marriage was an arranged marriage," Karim said, sitting back down on the bed next to Rachel, "but he prefers being married to my mother. He says American women are more lively."

"Right," Rachel said. "Definitely."

At that she got up and started doing her cheerleading routine, bending and kicking and jumping around. "I would die before I'd be a cheerleader," Laurie said with a grim expression when Rachel was done.

"Why?" Karim asked, surprised.

"Because the whole thing is to get boys all excited. It's so dumb!"

Rachel collapsed on the bed, panting. "That's *not* the whole thing." She took another sip of champagne. "It's an art. Not everybody can do it. And anyhow, getting them excited is the *point*. Then they play better and they win."

"I'm not saying no one should do it," Laurie said. "Just that I never would."

"My mother used to be a cheerleader," Karim said.

Rachel looked puzzled. "Do they have them in Saudi Arabia? I thought they had this thing about women not showing their bodies."

"My mother's from Texas," Karim said.

"Oh, right. . . . After he dumped the Arab ones, he took her on?"

Karim looked shocked. "He didn't dump them. He got divorced."

Rachel leaned against Karim and closed her eyes. "That's just an American expression," she murmured, kissing him.

At one o'clock Boyce drove us all home. He let Rachel off first. Just as she was getting out, she leaned over and whispered into my ear, "I pretended he was you."

Laurie looked at me. "What'd she say?"

"Just that she had a good time at the concert."

"So, why'd she have to whisper?"

I shrugged.

"If you ever stoop so low as to go after her, I'm going to *kill* you!" Laurie said.

"She's a fool," I said, kissing Laurie.

"A fool with huge boobs who'd probably let you do anything you wanted with her," Laurie hissed.

I wished she hadn't put it that way. Because after Laurie was left off and Boyce drove me home, I started imagining that. I closed my eyes, and Rachel and Laurie and all five of the Go-Go's kind of blended into a bunch of wonderful girls who couldn't get enough of me. Boyce had to say twice, "Evan, we've arrived at your home."

I opened my eyes and came to. "Thanks, Boyce. See you around."

Normally I would enjoy getting out of a Rolls in front of our building, but no one was around to watch.

5

ONCE A MONTH I CALL MY FATHER. HIS NAME is Julian and he runs a TV-and-stereo store in Tampa, Florida. For about five years, after he and Mom were divorced, he was married to a skinny red-haired woman named Lillian, but she left him last year. It's always a downer to talk to my father. I feel guilty even thinking that. I knew he wanted to get custody of us, but he lost the case and that makes him really bitter about life in general, but especially about Mom. That's one reason he says he moved so far away. If he couldn't see us all the time, he decided it would be less painful to see us just once a year. That doesn't make such good sense to me, but it was his decision.

"So, how's it going, Evan?" he asked.

"It's going well."

"How's your girlfriend?" He knows about Laurie. He's even met her.

"She's fine. We went to a rock concert last night, the Go-Go's."

"She hasn't cast her eye elsewhere?"

"Not yet." My father has this theory that women always desert men just when they need them most. I think that might be based on my mother, but the thing is, my father *can* be sort of depressing to be around. If *I* were married to him, I might have cast my eye elsewhere too. "How about you?"

"What about me?"

"You said last time you met a nice lady. I forget her name."

"Alice?"

"I don't remember."

"She was just passing through," my father said, sighing. "Now I'm alone again, business is slow, the usual."

"That's too bad," I said.

"I've been reading the philosophers. That's my main consolation. *Amor fati*. Do you know what that means?"

"Nope."

"*Love what is*—that's the answer, Evan. Don't go hoping for wonderful things to happen. Just enjoy life with all its flat, painful, trivial details, because when you come right down to it, that's all there is."

"Yeah, well . . . I guess that's true."

"*Amor fati*. . . . You write that down and put it over your desk."

"Okay, I will."

"How's your brother? Still racking up the grades?"

"Yeah. . . . He only got a 92 in chemistry, though."

"I was like him," my father said. "Incredible grades. They said I was a genius. Entered college at sixteen. What good did it do me? There's more to life than good grades."

"I know," I said. I believe that.

"*Amor fati*. . . . You keep that in mind, and it'll help."

"Okay, Dad, I will. . . . Take care."

"You, too. . . . I love you, Evan."

"Same here."

Boy, there is nothing in the whole *world* that can get me as depressed as a conversation with my father! I think I'd rather get a call saying I'd been inducted into the army or expelled from school. I'm not going to write *amor fati* down and put it over my desk because I don't think it's true! There's a lot more to life than flat, painful, trivial details! Just because my father's life didn't work out the way he wanted doesn't mean *mine* won't. First of all, girls like me. I have a good personality and I'm good-looking. He may have entered college at sixteen, but he was always a funny-looking, strange kid. I mean, Harold is funny-looking and strange, but he still seems to get a kick out of life. My father just kind of lies there like some dog stretched out in the middle of the road waiting to be run over. I *am* going to hope for wonderful things to happen to me. That doesn't mean I'll just lie there, daydreaming for the rest of my life. I'll try and make them happen. I think that's a better philosophy than *amor fati*.

"Did you call your father, Evan?" Mom asked at dinner.

"Yeah, I did," She always reminds me, even though I almost never forget.

"How is he?"

It's funny. I feel bad saying anything negative about my father, even just admitting the way I really feel, to anyone, even to Gary, who I think feels pretty much the same. It's kind of like it would be betraying him, though you could say who am I fooling? "He's well."

"I wish Lillian would stop calling me," Mom said. "I just don't want to hear any more long sad stories about her life with Julian." She looked sidelong at Harold. "If *your* ex-wife ever calls, tell her I'm in the shower."

"My ex-wife doesn't even remember she's my ex-wife," Harold said. "She's on to new and better things. She married a sixty-four-year-old geologist with a bad heart and a stock portfolio, and I imagine they're happy as clams."

"I told them a little bit about the concert, and then my mother turned to Gary and said, "Hon, have you decided yet about the Senior Prom? Are you going?"

"Probably not," Gary said gloomily.

"Why not? Don't you like anyone enough to ask them?"

There was a pause.

"Yeah, well, there's someone I sort of like," Gary said.

"So, ask her!" my mother said. "She'll probably be tickled pink."

"Well, for one thing, she doesn't go to Haines," Gary said.

"Where's she from?"

"She lives in Brooklyn, She takes bassoon lessons from Mrs. Maraketti."

"You mean that lovely dark-haired girl who played the duet with you last year?"

Gary nodded.

"I'm sure she'd *love* to go! . . . Why not ask her at least?"

Gary stabbed his mashed potatoes with a fork. "I've never even asked her on a regular date," he said dolefully.

"What's stopping you?" My mother looked puzzled.

Gary just sort of shrugged.

Harold said, "Sweetie, you don't understand the delicacy of the male ego. One *tiny* bruise, one slight, and we go into a downward spiral that may take decades to undo. Men have entered the priesthood at twenty just after being turned down by one dark-haired, golden-throated bassoonist."

"*I'm* not like that," I said. "I've gotten turned down lots of times. What's the big deal? You just ask someone else."

"Boy, they ought to clone your ego and put it on display at the Smithsonian," Gary said sarcastically.

"It's not a matter of ego," I said. "I just figure there are a lot of nice girls and if you don't get one, you'll get another one."

Harold raised his glass. "To nice girls everywhere, whether they play the bassoon or not."

"I still think you should ask her," Mom said. "What's her name?"

Gary looked dreamy, almost the way Karim does when he looks at Rachel. "Alexandra Silvanovitz."

At school the next week Karim said he called Rachel and asked her out, but she said she only liked to double-date. She said she thought she was too young to get serious about anyone, but if Laurie and I wanted to double again, that was fine. That was discouraging, because Laurie doesn't like Rachel and I'd just set it up that way to give Karim a start. "I may start lifting weights," he said.

"Why?"

"I'm too thin," Karim said. "If I were strong, I think Rachel would look at me differently. . . . Or do you think it's my being from another culture?"

I personally think it's because Rachel is an airhead, but I just shrugged. "It can't hurt, Kar."

6

IN SOCIAL STUDIES CLASS, MS. BOORSTEIN HAS been teaching us about women's rights, how they had to fight to get the vote and other things. "But there are many areas in which feminists feel things are still not equal," she said. "For instance, I cut this clipping out of the newspaper, since it concerns an area of interest to many of you—high school sports. . . . 'NOW, the National Organization for Women, has lodged a formal protest about the fact that there are no cheerleading teams to support girls' sports, like basketball and softball. Cheerleading is part of what helps teams win,' Mrs. Hess said. 'It arouses school spirit. We feel all New York schools should make an effort to recruit girls to support their own teams as well as boys' teams. That would show real equality.'" She looked around the room. "How many of you girls are cheerleaders?"

A bunch of girls raised their hands.

"Well, what do you girls think? Would you like to do your cheers for the girls' teams as well as the boys'?"

Rachel raised her hand. "I don't think that would make any sense, Ms. Boorstein."

"Why not, Rachel?"

"Well, part of the point of cheerleading is to get the guys, well, excited, so they really want to win. Girls wouldn't get excited."

Ms. Boorstein looked over at the boys. "Is that the purpose of cheerleading in your eyes, boys? How about you, Marlon? I hear you're a star on the softball team."

Marlon cleared his throat. "Yeah, well, it's kind of a tradition. We're working hard, doing our best on the field, and the cheerleaders are doing their best to encourage us. So, it's sort of like real life where women tell their husbands they're doing a good job at work an make them good meals and stuff."

At that Laurie and her best friend, Arlene, yelled out simultaneously, "Boo! Hiss! Sexist!"

Ms. Boorstein smiled. "Why do you girls feel Marlon's remarks was sexist?"

"Are you kidding?" Arlene said. She's a chubby girl with black crinkly hair and glasses. "In real life, women work just as hard as men. Who cheers *them* on?"

"You mean taking care of babies?" Willy said.

"No, dumbhead, I mean, earning a living and being a lawyer or a doctor or a taxidermist, like my mom. Who cheers *her* on?"

"Your father?" Willy suggested.

Arlene rolled her eyes. "Sure. From Whitefish, Montana, where he's living with his twenty-two-year-old girlfriend and not even sending us alimony checks half the time?"

"Arlene, I think maybe we're getting a little off the topic here," Ms. Boorstein said, "but I do think you've brought up an interesting point. We would all agree, I think, that cheerleading serves an important function. It helps the team feel someone is rooting for them. The question is, don't girls' teams need that encouragement too?"

Laurie waved her hand in the air. "Yeah, we do," she said. "But we don't want some airhead girls with big boobs and pompons cheering us on, I can tell you that. That would just make us lose!"

"But that's what cheerleading *is*," Marlon said.

"Then we don't want it," said Arlene.

"Well, *we* don't want to do it except for the boys' teams," said Rachel haughtily, "so you don't have to worry about it."

Another cheerleader, Goldie Fisher, said, "Ms. Boorstein, I think what Laurie said is wrong. Cheerleaders don't all have big breasts. Some of us are good at it just the way other girls are good at ballet or gymnastics—because we're graceful and well coordinated."

It was mean, but when Goldie said that cheerleaders don't have big breasts, a lot of the boys began to snicker, because Goldie is about as flat as we are.

"I'm on your side there," Ms. Boorstein said. "I was a cheerleader once myself, and as I recall, it was damn hard work. And I was never spectacularly endowed myself. . . . However, I just wanted to float one suggestion, since I gather most of you girls agree with Rachel that you don't want to cheerlead for the girls' team: How about some of you boys cheerleading for the girls' team?"

There was a dead silence.

"Hey, that's a great idea!" Arlene said. "Right on, Ms. Boorstein!"

Marlon looked totally disgusted. "That's absurd," he said. "It's impossible."

"Why is it impossible?" Mrs. Boorstein asked.

"Because it's not something boys do. . . . What boy is going to get up with pompons on his wrists and kick his legs in the air and make an ass of himself . . . unless he's gay or something?"

Ms. Boorstein looked all around the room. "Is that the only way cheerleading can be done?"

Suddenly I had an idea. It was like one of those moments in a movie when the hero sees God and goes down the aisle. I raised my hand. Ms. Boorstein said, "You've been unusually silent today, Evan. What do *you* think?"

"I'd like to be a cheerleader for the girls' team," I said. "I think they're right. They need someone to cheer them on, but it would make more sense if it was a bunch of guys. It wouldn't have to be sissy. We could work up our own routines."

Ms. Boorstein smiled. "Well, that certainly is a radical proposal. How about the rest of you boys? Evan has taken the first brave step. Do any of you want to join him?"

I looked around the room. All the boys were looking

at their feet. Suddenly Karim raised his hand. "I'd like to be a male cheerleader too," he said.

"Wonderful," said Ms. Boorstein. "Anyone else?"

Marlon cleared his throat. "It's not a matter of bravery, Ms. Boorstein. If you're on the team, you don't have time to be a cheerleader as well."

"That may apply to you, Marlon, but surely not to all the boys in this room."

"Yeah, but a lot of us have after-school things like chess or walking the dog," Milo said. He's skinny and wears glasses and is captain of the chess team.

"It's more a political issue," Willy put in. "It's always been one way, girls cheering for boys, so why suddenly try and change it?"

"Why try to free the slaves?" Arlene yelled. "Why given women the vote?"

Marlon laughed. "Maybe that wasn't such a wise idea."

Just then the bell rang. I got up, feeling a little uncertain about what I had done. Once you do something like that, you can't go back on it. The die is cast, as Harold sometimes says. What softened the blow was Laurie's coming over and throwing her arms around me. "Are you really going to do it?" she asked. "Did you really mean it?"

"Sure," I said. "We'll do a better job than any girls' cheerleading group ever did. We'll be the best."

Rachel said, "Evan, I don't think you realize how much work cheerleading is. It takes skill, too. Not just *anyone* can do it."

I beamed at her. "I'm the man for the job. I have

skill, I work hard, I'm innovative. . . . What more do you want?"

Arlene shook my hand. "You're a great guy, Evan. They ought to clone you and pitch the rest of these dumbos out to sea."

Karim had been standing quietly by my side. Rachel had just ignored him. But Arlene said, "That's terrific that you're going to do it too, Karim. The two of you will make an excellent team."

Karim turned red, but he looked pleased.

That evening I was going to have dinner at Laurie's house. It was her birthday, but she decided she didn't want a party. Her mother said she'd cook anything Laurie wanted, so Laurie said she wanted lobster and artichokes, with strawberry shortcake for dessert. It was a fantastic meal. All of us, even Laurie's six-year-old brother, Ranger, got an entire lobster. We all got lobster crackers, too. It was a real struggle getting the lobsters open. I helped Laurie, and her mother helped Ranger. There was a bowl of melted butter right in front of each of us.

While we were eating, Laurie told everyone about me starting a boys' cheerleading team. "Ther's only two of them so far," she said, "but Evan's so charismatic, I bet they'll all going to want to do it in the end."

The thing with Laurie is that she knows just what to say to make me feel wonderful. It isn't just a matter of buttering me up. I've always liked that word *charismatic*. It sounds almost like it means having magic powers.

"Have you given any thought to *how* you'll do it?"

Laurie's father asked. He's a plump, gray-haired man who's going bald.

"Not yet, but I will." I know Laurie's father thinks she's too young to be going out so much with one person, so I always feel sort of insecure around him, wanting to show him I'm trustworthy.

Ranger was going around putting stickers on everyone, to give them names. Laurie was Op, her mother was Lop, her father was Top. "What do *you* want to be?" he asked me.

"Zop?" I suggested.

"Is that a real word?"

"I don't think so."

He attached a sticker with ZOP on it to my shirt. Then he started putting sticker names on all the lobsters. Laurie thinks he gets too much attention because her parents waited so long to have a boy and when they finally had one were ecstatic.

"I never knew city schools made such a big deal out of sports," Laurie's mother said. She looks basically like Laurie's father, except she's prettier and not bald. "I went to school in New York, and I don't remember sports being that important. I didn't even hear of cheerleaders till I was out of college."

"They weren't important to you, dear," Laurie's father said, "but they were important." He sighed.

I guess he wasn't that good at sports.

After dinner Laurie and I went into her room. We talked and listened to the new record I got her for her birthday and made out a little. Laurie has a lock on her door, but Ranger is always pounding on it saying he needs scissors or some Scotch tape. Laurie screams at him to bug off, but usually a minute later her mother comes around saying, "Dear, he *only* needs the Scotch tape. . . . Couldn't you open the door for just a minute?" I don't know if she does that to check up on us or what, but it can really be annoying.

"I felt so proud of you," Laurie said. "I was scared Ms. Boorstein was going to make Rachel and all of them cheerlead for our team. It's hard to be the only one volunteering for something. I would've been too scared."

"Well, I figure you've got to start somewhere," I said.

"At least you've got Karim," Laurie said. "Maybe cheerleading will get his mind off Rachel."

"Maybe," I said, but as Harold says, I wouldn't bet the ranch on it.

7

DESPITE LAURIE'S ENCOURAGEMENT, I FELT really uncomfortable about the whole cheerleading idea the more I thought about it. Usually I like to think things out before I volunteer to do them, or at least have some idea in my mind of how I can do it. And I knew Karim wasn't going to be any help at all, since he doesn't know the first thing about cheerleading. He was looking to me to plan the whole thing and put it into execution. I didn't want to let him down and I didn't want to let Laurie down, but whenever I started thinking about it in earnest, I got paralyzed.

When I got home from school the next day, no one was there. I hadn't told any of my family about cheerleading, because I wanted to first make sure I was definitely going to do it. As I started into my room to figure out what to do, the phone rang. It was a girl. "Is Gary there?"

Girls never call my brother up, whereas, I sometimes get three or four calls a night. You could say, if you wanted to be unkind, that despite his wonderful grades, he's somewhat retarded socially. "No, he's out now," I said. "Can I take a message?" I'm great on the phone. I can do anything on the phone, even change my voice different ways, depending on the effect I want to create.

"This is Alexandra Silvanovitz. I just wanted to tell Gary that our rehearsal has been postponed till next Friday at four. Can you tell him that?"

"Sure." Alexandra Silvanovitz? it sounded familiar. Then I remembered. She was the one Gary liked, the one he wanted to invite to the Senior Prom. "This is Evan. I'm Gary's brother."

"Yes, I know," Alexandra said. "I think we met after the concert last year."

I couldn't exactly remember, but I had gotten another brainstorm. "Do you, uh, go out, Alexandra?"

"Not a whole lot," Alexandra said. "I assume you mean with boys?"

"Right."

"I'm very serious about my music and I go to an all-girls' school, so there aren't that many opportunities." She laughed. "I think I might be a little old for you, Evan. I'm seventeen."

"No, it's Gary."

"Yes?"

"See, the thing is, he likes you . . . a lot, only he's

scared to ask you out. Not so much scared, but shy. He hasn't had that much experience with girls."

"Oh. . . . What makes you think he likes me?"

"Well, he was talking about it at dinner, how he wanted to ask you to the Senior Prom only he'd never asked you on a regular date so he wasn't sure how to go about it."

"Why doesn't he ask me on a regular date, then?"

"That's what we all said. But, like I said, he has kind of a fragile ego. He's scared you'll say no."

"I wouldn't," Alexandra said softly.

"Would you say yes?"

"Definitely."

I thought a little more. "Well, the thing is, he still doesn't know that and I can't tell him because he'd kill me if he knew we'd had this conversation, so what I was wondering was, maybe you could ask *him* out."

"Would he say yes?"

"He might even faint with excitement. Yeah, I can guarantee absolutely he'd say yes."

There was a pause. "Well, actually I do have these two tickets for a Judith LeClair concert on Saturday. I was going to go with my aunt, but if you really think he would—"

"It would really make his whole year," I said. "Basically, all he does is study and play the bassoon and that's not such a healthy life for a seventeen-year-old guy. My mother's quite worried about him, actually." That's not really true, but sometimes you have to lay it on thick to make your point.

"Gary's so good-looking," Alexandra said. "It's really sweet that he doesn't know it."

"Yeah, well, tastes differ, I guess. His personality may turn some girls off."

"I think his personality is wonderful! I hate that whole macho boasting thing. I've always liked shy, sensitive men. In fact, Gary is sort of my ideal of the perfect man."

Boy, this girl must really be hard up! "Okay, well, great. . . . Only, Alexandra, could you, like, even if you end up getting married someday, never tell Gary we had this phone conversation? Because it might shorten my life considerably."

"I promise. This was really sweet of you, Evan. Gary's certainly lucky to have such a sensitive brother."

I hope Gary will look at it that way. Actually, it was a good deed. Left to his own devices, Gary might never even go out with anyone. I bet I've had ten times more experience with girls than he has, and I'm just fourteen. Of course, I may be unusual in the opposite direction.

But at dinner I began wondering if Gary was worth doing a good deed for. "God, I heard the craziest rumor today in school," he said. "Someone said you and that Arab guy are going to dress up as cheerleaders for the girls' softball team? What is this? *Tootsie* or something?"

"We're not going to dress up like girl cheerleaders," I said. "We're going to be boy cheerleaders."

He rolled his eyes. "Gimme a break, Evan. Wait till I graduate at least, will you?"

"What does that have to do with it?" Mom asked.

"I'm a senior. I don't want my last year of school to

be ruined by my brother's hamming it up just to get attention in some idiotic way."

I felt like calling Alexandra Silvanovitz back and telling her it was all a total act and that Gary was really an insensitive jerk. "I'm doing it because Laurie's on the team and she thinks it's only fair since the boys' teams have girl cheerleaders."

"What if she told you to paint yourself blue and do somersaults down the hall, would you do *that*, too? Don't you have a mind of your own?"

I turned red. I could have killed him, I felt so angry. "It was *my* idea, not Laurie's."

"You're actually going to get out there in little pink skirts and boots and twirl batons?"

"No! I told you. I'm going to work up a routine with Kar, a *boy's* routine."

"What kind of routine?"

"We haven't planned it out yet."

Gary looked at Mom. "Don't you even care? Next thing he'll be wearing ankle bracelets and purple eye-shadow. Everyone'll think he's gay. It's a good thing I'll be away at college next year."

"Gary, I think you're being shockingly prejudiced," Mom said. "We should all be very proud of Evan for doing something like this."

Boy, that was a great moment. Mom almost never takes my side against Gary. She claims it's because she thinks I'm so secure and he isn't. Just as I was beaming from ear to ear, Harold added, "And what's all this junk about gays? Some of my best friends are gay."

"Yeah?" Gary said defensively. "Which ones?"

"None of your damn business," Harold snapped.

That was interesting. I never knew any of Mom and Harold's friends were gay.

Gary got up from the table. "Well, all I can say is, if either of you went to our school, you'd feel a lot differently. If he at least had another name, I wouldn't mind so much."

"What's wrong with Evan?" I said, pretending to be innocent. "I think it's a good name."

"I mean our last name," Gary said. "I don't want anyone to know we're related."

As he stomped out of the room I said, "Tell them I'm adopted!"

After he left, there was a silence. Basically I felt pretty good about Mom and Harold's taking my side, but I still felt angry at Gary. It's painful to have your older brother think you're a disgrace. And I'm not as sure of myself as Mom likes to believe. A lot of times I just act secure, but what's going on underneath is totally different. For instance, right now, I have to admit, if I could go back to that day in class and undo the whole thing, I would in a second. But I can't, and I'm too chicken to go back on my word now.

"You know, it's strange with Gary," Mom said thoughtfully. "In so many ways he's so mature for his age, but sometimes he acts really childish."

"He's just threatened," Harold said. "At his age, guys are really uncertain about thier sexual identity, especially if they haven't had much experience with girls."

"Do you think that's it?" Mom said.

Harold went over and rumpled her hair. "Sure, don't worry, hon. . . . And don't *you* worry either, Evan."

"*I'm* not worried, I said coolly.

A couple of minutes later the phone rang. Harold answered it and then yelled for Gary. After Gary had taken it in his room, Harold said. "Well, God was listening. It's a girl."

Mom's eyes brightened. "A girl? Which one?"

"Alexandra Silvanovitz."

Mom actually leaped out of the chair. "That's the girl he likes! Oh, this is wonderful! Oh, let her like him!"

Despite hating Gary with all my heart, I got a kind of satisfaction out of this, knowing I'd masterminded the whole thing and no one would ever know, least of all the victim himself. A few minutes later Gary wandered back in, looking totally pleased with himself. "Well, I guess I'll have to bow out of the dinner on Saturday," he said. "Alexandra wondered if I could go to a Judith LeClair concert with her."

"How marvelous!" Mom exclaimed. "Go, go, by all means! We don't mind, do we Harold?"

"Who's Judith LeClair?" I asked.

"Just the greatest bassoonist of this century," Gary said. "I'm amazed she could get tickets."

"Well, I'm just delighted that we live in an era in which girls can take the initiative when they like a boy. It's so much healthier," Mom said.

"You took the initiative with *me*," Harold said.

"I did?" Mom looked surprised. "In what way?"

"You came up to me after I'd been playing doubles

and said, 'I've never met anyone who has as bad a backhand as I do and can still get it over the net.' I was smitten from then on."

For some reason Mom blushed. "How awful! God, did I really say something that inept?"

"I knew you were just too overwhelmed to admit how you really felt," Harold said.

While they were beaming at each other, I snuck a look at Gary. He was gazing off into space, dreaming of Alexandra. *Quel* jerk, as Laurie would say.

FOR THE NEXT WEEK OR SO KARIM AND I TOOK a lot of ribbing at school about our having offered to be cheerleaders. I think I took a lot more because I had been the one to set the thing up and everyone assumed, correctly, that Karim was just doing it because I was. What made it harder was that Karim was doing it because he assumed anything I decided to do would add to his standing in the class. Sometimes you do terrific things that you want everyone to know about and no one knows, and then along comes a thing like this which you feel really mixed about and by nightfall there isn't a person or a teacher, even, in the entire school who doesn't know.

At lunchtime a tenth grader who's on the swimming team with me, Nathan Katz, came over and said, "We thought maybe you'd both like copies of this." He handed

Karim and me copies of "The Gay Rights Newsletter," which he and some of his friends distribute.

After he walked away, Karim looked at me, puzzled. "Why should we be interested in this?"

I sighed. "I guess he assumes we might be gay."

"Why?"

"Well, just because we're doing something girls normally do. It's hard to explain. . . . And some kids think we're going to dress up as girl cheerleaders."

Karim looked really uncomfortable. "That isn't what you had in mind, is it?"

"No, but you know how it is with rumors."

At the end of the day we were hanging out in front of the school, when Marlon and Milo walked by. "Bought your pompons yet, Evan?" Marlon asked.

"Yeah, we can't wait to see you do the splits." He and Milo doubled over.

Karim invited me over to his house for dinner. When we got there, I was feeling really low again. "We may have made a big mistake," I said.

"In what way?" Karim couldn't believe I made mistakes.

"I wonder if this cheerleading thing is such a great idea."

"But you said it was only fair since the girls cheerlead for the boys' teams."

"It is . . . but I don't know if I want to be the one to do it."

Karim was silent for a long moment. "You think we'll be laughingstocks?"

"Sort of," I admitted.

Karim looked at me for a long moment. "Then I will do it alone," he said.

"You will?"

"Yes. Because my father has explained many times how we came to this country because here they have equal rights for all people, including women, and how you must fight for those rights and not take them for granted."

"True." You learn all that stuff at school, but I never thought of anyone taking it seriously. "No, listen, I'll do it, Kar. I was just telling you how I feel deep down. What we need to do is think about *how*, so it doesn't strike anyone as sissyish."

Karim's family eats in this large living-dining room which is about the size of our apartment-house lobby. There's a terrace all around it where you can see all over New York. There's a servant in a uniform who brings the food around two times and waits while you help yourself, even if it's just hamburgers and potato chips. The first couple of times I ate there, the whole thing made me really uncomfortable, but now I'm basically used to it.

Karim explained to his parents about the cheerleading plan. His father looked puzzled. "Is that legal? For boys?" Mr. Shahbaz is a small, very neat man who usually wears white suits and has a big diamond ring on one hand. I've never seen a man wear a ring like that. He also has a black beard and big black eyes, like Karim's.

"Sure, it's legal," I said. "It's just rare. No one's ever done it in our school before."

"You will be innovators?" he said.

I nodded.

Mr. Shahbaz looked approving. "You're like your father, Karim. I, too, have always been an innovator. And that's why we have all this—" He made a sweeping gesture. "I took to modern ways. I didn't become mired in the past, like *my* father."

I had always thought in Saudi Arabia they just kind of handed out oil wells when you were born, they had so many of them. I never thought of the fact that it was like a business and not everyone might be good at it.

"So, how're you going to do it?" Susie said. Mrs. Shahbaz says I should call her Susie, so I do because she looks like a Susie more than like a Mrs. Shahbaz. She's little and blond and perky and has a slight Southern accent.

"We don't know," Karim admitted.

"The main thing is, we don't want it to be sissyish," I added.

"Cheerleading *isn't* sissyish!" Susie exclaimed. "It's work! I was a star cheerleader in high school, and believe me, I never worked harder in my life! I used to lose five pounds every game."

"What kinds of routines did you do?" Karim asked.

"Let me see, it's so long ago." Suddenly she jumped up. "Okay, y'all just wait here, and I'll be back in a minute with a surprise. You go right on eating."

We did. Mr. Shahbaz didn't seem that excited. He never does. He always speaks in a really slow, calm voice. About five minutes later Susie came running back into the room. She was wearing a short, short white skirt, halter top, and little boots, and she was carrying a silver-tipped baton. "All right, here goes! Now, remember, y'all, I'm a little out of practice." Then she went through this whole number, jumping, shouting, twirling her baton. The first time she dropped the baton, she said, "Darn. I never was good at that. Those things are so slippery."

I figure Susie is somewhere in her thirties, like my mother, but I have to say this, she certainly has an excellent figure and a lot of energy. I can't imagine my mother even *trying* a routine like that, and if I thought of Laurie's mother, the idea would be even more laughable. When Susie was done and had collapsed, panting, in a chair, Mr. Shahbaz called loudly: "Bravo! Magnificent! This is a true American art form."

Susie looked pleased. "Y'all should have seen me in my prime. I've slowed down lots."

"You were superb," Karim said proudly.

"Yeah, you're a lot better than some of the girls at our school," I complimented her.

"I used to practice every day, two solid *hours*," Susie said. "If I gained one pound, I skipped lunch the next day. The coach used to weigh us in and if we were one pound over, out! No mercy!"

"Do you think we should do a routine like that?" Karim asked her.

Susie frowned. "Well, I don't think so, honey. That's a girls' routine. You need a boys' routine. What're you planning on wearing?"

We shrugged.

She squinted her eyes. "You know, I just had an idea.

Remember that rock group we saw in London last year, the way they had on skintight leather pants and those sequiny silver shirts? How about something along that line?"

I thought of Mike Hutchence and how those girls had clung to him like bees cling to a flower, kissing him all over. "That would be great," I said, "only how would we do that?"

"I'll make them for you." She looked excited. "I've done menswear for two years now. They'll be custom-made outfits. We can—"

"I think leather pants will be too hot," Karim said, "if we have to move around a lot."

"Maybe leather shorts?" Susie said. "Or just a lighter-weight fabric that looks like leather? I think you want to look kind of macho and sexy, even a little bit menacing."

I liked that idea a lot. There was definitely nothing sissyish about it.

After dinner Karim and I went back to his room. We were both feeling about a thousand times better. The idea of looking like rock stars made a big difference. "How about your drums?" Karim said. "Could you still play them?"

"Sure, but how? You mean while you're doing the cheers?"

"Exactly. You drum the beat and call out the cheer, and we both do the routine. We wouldn't have to do that with all of them, just a few."

As I took the bus home I was beginning to feel a little bit better. *Innovators*, that's what we were. *Charismatic* innovators.

EVERY APRIL MY FATHER COMES TO NEW York. He comes then partly because, according to him, it's a slow time for his business—though as far as I can tell, most times are slow—and also because Gary and I both have birthdays in April. Not on the same day. Mine is April second and his is April eighteenth.

My father always stays in a hotel and takes us out to eat or to a show if there's anything special we want to see. This year when he called we got on different extensions, like we always do. "If you have any girlfriends you want to bring along, that's fine with me," he said.

There was a slight pause. On the one hand, I'd like to bring Laurie because she likes getting dressed up and going to fancy places. But I'm never sure how my father will act. Gary said, "There is someone I'd like to bring. . . . Her name's Alexandra."

"Wonderful, I'd love to meet her. How about you, Evan? One of your many admirers?"

"I'll bring Laurie," I said. "You met her once, remember?"

"Of course I remember. Well, I'm glad to see you boys haven't been damaged by your father's experiences. Not all of the male sex are losers when it comes to women. Some, so I've heard, are winners."

"You're not a loser, Dad," I said.

"You're kind, Ev. Don't interview any of the ladies that've passed through my life. But I guess you don't need to do that. You've probably heard enough horror stories from Holly to set your hair on end."

My father has this idea that my mother has been sitting around since the day he left ten years ago doing nothing but telling us what a louse he was. In fact, about all she's ever said is she thought it was unfair of him to try and get sole custody of us when she'd been an excellent mother. She said she would have been glad to let him have joint custody, but I guess he wanted all or nothing.

"So, where should we meet?" Gary asked.

My father gave us the name of a Chinese restaurant in the Fifties. He knows we both like Chinese food. When we hung up, I went into the hall where Gary was. "It ought to be a good meal," I said.

"Why does he say things like that?" Gary exploded.

"About Mom, and about being a loser? Why doesn't he have any pride?"

I shrugged. "It's his personality, I guess."

"I mean, so he can't get a girlfriend? That isn't being a loser, necessarily. There are other things in life besides women."

I don't know. Gary may feel that way, but I think if I didn't have a girlfriend I'd be pretty depressed. "What do you think he does?" I asked. "I mean, why do they stop liking him?"

"Self-pity," Gary said. "I mean, would *you* want to be married to him?"

I laughed. "No, but I wouldn't want to be married to Harold either, especially."

"Harold is what he is, and he isn't ashamed of it," Gary said. "The guy's ten times weirder than Dad in some ways, but he doesn't spend all his time apologizing and trying to make you feel sorry for him."

This was one of the first conversations I'd ever had with Gary about Dad. I felt a lot better, since before, I thought it was maybe just me who felt this way. "Did he tell you about *amor fati*?" I said.

Gary gave a deep sign and intoned, "Life is just an endless stream of trivial painful details and there's no need to expect any more out of it. Will you promise me you'll put that over your desk, son?"

I laughed. I usually hate it when Gary imitates me, but he had my father's tone of voice down pat. "I don't even believe that," I said.

"God, no," Gary said. "I'm going to be somebody

worth something and if I'm not, I'm going to shut up about it."

"Me, too," I agreed.

Maybe every ten years or so Gary and I will have a good conversation about something. That means the next one will come when I'm twenty-four and he's twenty-eight. I wonder what we'll talk about then? Who we're married to? The terrific job we have? It's hard to imagine that far ahead. Hey, maybe my father will even have found some nice lady who'll love him the way he is, a female Harold. No, it's hard to imagine a female Harold. Impossible, actually.

Gary was going to pick up Alexandra at her house, and I was going to pick up Laurie. Then we were going to meet Dad at the restaurant, The House of Chan. There're lots of little Chinese places along Broadway, near where we live, but this is a big fancy one where they bring finger bowls and give you fresh pineapple all carved out in its shell for dessert. It's my favorite restaurant.

Laurie looked pretty. Her hair was kind of shiny and a little spiked out, but not too extreme. She had eye makeup on, which makes her eyes look huge, like a raccoon's, and she had on slacks and her Go-Go's T-shirt. "Is this fancy enough?" she asked.

"You look great," I said.

"Sometimes fathers can be sort of conservative is why I wondered," she said. "Daddy spent an *hour* trying to get me into a dress. I said to him, 'Daddy, if dresses are so great, why don't *you* wear them?' And then, just when I got done with *him*, Mom starts in on how come

I have to wear two different earrings? It's boring to wear two of the same kind! Do they expect me to look like *them*? Should I dye my hair gray and gain fifty pounds too?"

"No, never," I said, taking her hand. "You're perfect right now."

"Even my figure?" Laurie asked. "You don't wish there was more of it?"

This is where my skills as a diplomat come in. I said, "It isn't amount. It's shape and where they're placed and—"

Laurie gave a snort of laughter. "You mean they aren't always placed here? Some girls have them in back or on the side?"

"I just meant, they're in proportion," I said. "That's what counts."

She kissed me on the lips, which always gives me a thrill, even if her lip gloss comes off on me. Laurie may not have the most on top of any girl her age, but her lips are the best: soft and round and wonderful. Any boy my age would give up a lot to kiss Laurie.

When we got to the restaurant, Dad was there with Gary and Alexandra.

"Hi, Evan," Alexandra said. "I think we've met before." She smiled at me as though to say she knew we had a secret and she'd never give it away. What can I say about Alexandra Silvanovitz? She looks like a girl who plays the bassoon and likes my brother. No, that's not fair. Objectively, I'd say she's in between pretty and not, with a long nose and brown hair parted in the middle, held back with barrettes. She had on the kind of dress Laurie's parents probably wished she had worn, dark blue with long sleeves.

"Hi, Dad," I said, sliding in. It was a round table. "Sorry we're late."

"You look like twins," Alexandra said to us.

"Yeah, we like to dress alike," Laurie said.

I was wearing a Go-Go's shirt too, but I had on a jacket because I wasn't sure they'd let me in otherwise. I even had a tie in my pocket.

"Well, girls, go right ahead and order whatever suits your fancy," my father said. "This is the best Chinese restaurant in New York, some say in the world."

"Better than in China?" Laurie asked.

"I've never been to China," said my father.

"It might be like in pizza they don't eat Italy," Laurie said. She laughed. "I mean, in Italy they don't eat pizza, or at least not as much as we do here. That's what my mom says."

"I've never been to Italy either," my father said.

"Where have you been?" Laurie asked, unfolding her napkin.

My father sighed. "Nowhere."

She looked surprised. "Gee. . . . How come?"

"I'm a divorced man, I have two households to keep going, I'm not a millionaire, young lady. The reason we're at this restaurant is to celebrate Gary's and Evan's birthdays. Don't think I eat like this every day."

Laurie looked embarrassed, like she'd said the wrong thing. I wanted to tell her that with my father, any conversation you have can end up like that.

We ordered a lot—hot and sour soup, egg rolls,

barbecued spareribs, five main courses. "This is really delicious," Alexandra said. She ate delicately, taking small bites.

Laurie was gnawing on a sparerib. "Yeah, it's great." She had a pile of bones on the plate in front of her.

My father was just picking at his food. "I'm glad to see you young ladies have such hearty appetites," he said. "So many women are on diets all the time."

"I'm on a diet," Laurie said. "I'll just fast tomorrow. I've got to keep in shape because I'm on the softball team."

"And you," Dad said to Alexandra, "play the bassoon, I hear."

"Yes, I do," Alexandra said.

"Are you thinking of making that your profession?" he went on.

"I'm still not sure," Alexandra said. "I don't know if I have enough talent."

"Sure you do," Gary said. To the rest of us, he added, "She's the best."

"Not as good as you," Alexandra said.

They beamed at each other.

"Let me give you one piece of advice," my father said. "Never have two in a family with the same profession. It can only lead to disaster. I speak form experience."

I didn't exactly get that, because he sells stereos and Mom is a social worker. "Did Mom used to sell stereos?" I asked. It was hard to picture that, because she's not that mechanically minded.

"No, but I used to be a social worker," Dad said. "You boys never knew that. It was a depressing profession. No one ever really got better. Some just stopped coming or cured themselves. I couldn't take it."

"I can imagine that," Alexandra said.

"It's like life in general," Dad said. "Here we sit, the food isn't quite as good as remembered, the service is slow, for all we know the chef has just died and the restaurant's four stars may be taken away, you girls are wondering why your boyfriends have such a peculiar father. . . . Yet—and this is the key to it all—that's all there is! You will none of you ever be happier than you are *right now.*" He looked at all of us one by one with his baleful blue eyes. They always have gray patches underneath, like he hasn't slept all night.

"Really?" Laurie said, dismayed.

"*Amor fati,*" he went on. "Love what is. Don't go searching for the impossible. Don't berate your husbands for not being heroes of the silver screen. Don't go chasing rainbows. *Amor fati.* Will you remember that?"

I looked over at Gary. He was looking off into space as though my father didn't exist, in fact as though the whole restaurant didn't exist. I wish I could do that. I just felt horribly embarrassed. It was supposed to be a celebration of our birthdays, not a funeral!

Suddenly Laurie, who'd been looking down, exploded into laughter. It was like a volcano coming out and spilling over the table. She tried to cover her mouth, but the more she tried to stop, the more she couldn't. "Oh, I'm sorry," she gasped. "I'm sorry! This is terrible!"

When she finally calmed down, my father said, "What's so funny?"

"I thought—I was thinking *amor fati* sounded like it

ought to mean 'Love Fat People,' and that it would be a perfect slogan for Weight Watchers." She giggled again.

For a moment my father looked pained, but then he said, "It's true. We should love the fat, the lame, the diseased, the unfortunate. This is all quite true. . . . Evan, why are you squirming in your seat? Do you need to go to the bathroom?"

"Yeah," I said, jumping up, though I didn't really. Gary got up and went with me without saying anything.

"I think I'm going to murder him," he said when we were in the men's room.

"He can't help it," I said. "It's just his personality."

"What if Alexandra doesn't ever want to see me again?" He looked desperate. "I wouldn't blame her."

For a guy who claimed it didn't matter whether or not you had a girlfriend, he looked pretty anxious. "She'll still like you."

"Why did Mom marry him?" Gary went on, his voice rising. "Why is he our father?"

"That's just the way it is." Gary, though I wouldn't tell him this, is more like my father in that he always wants answers to huge philosophical issues. I'm more like Mom, more an everyday, practical kind of person.

We walked slowly back into the restaurant. Both of our girlfriends were sitting forward, listening to my father talk. As we came close, I heard Alexandra say, "I didn't know Tampa had burglaries just like here."

"It's worse than New York," my father said, spearing a chunk of lobster.

"Then why don't you move back?" Laurie asked.

"For what?" he demanded. "Here it's a jungle; there it's a jungle. Where is it *not* a jungle?"

"You could see Evan and Gary more, though," she said.

My father looked at the two of us. "Yes," he said sadly. "That's true. . . . but would they want that? Sometimes I get the feeling they wish I'd moved to Outer Mongolia."

Gary didn't say anything. He was probably thinking Outer Mongolia wasn't far away *enough*. But I said, "No, we'd like it, Dad. Really."

My father smiled. "He's a real politician, this kid. He could sell the Brooklyn Bridge to Mayor Koch. You better watch out, Laurie."

Laurie took my hand. "I can handle him," she said.

10

WHEN WE GOT BACK TO LAURIE'S APARTment it was eleven, but the place was totally quiet. Her parents often go to bed at ten, even on weekends. We went into Laurie's room. I was feeling sort of discombobulated, not exactly sorry I'd brought Laurie along, but hoping she hadn't minded.

"I'm sorry I made so many dumb remarks," she said, sitting down on the floor. "'In pizza they don't eat Italy.' 'Love fat people.'" She sighed.

"I was glad," I admitted. "At least it added some comic relief."

"I kept thinking he must think Alexandra is the perfect person for you or your brother to be dating and I'm some kind of spaced-out weirdo."

"Who cares what he thinks?"

"*I* care," Laurie said. "Don't *you* care what my father thinks of you?"

"*Your* father is a normal human being."

Laurie looked taken aback. "I didn't think your father was so bad. He's sort of sweet in a funny way. But why is he so sad?"

I shrugged.

"You're so cheerful and regular," she said.

"I guess I'm more like my mother."

"That's funny," Laurie said. "*I'm* more like my father. Maybe that's why we get along." She kissed me.

After that we kissed for a long time. Laurie has a million kinds of kisses, maybe because she doesn't want to do much besides kiss. I don't mind, but some of them can get me feeling pretty worked up. At one point she pulled back and said, "I decided for your birthday we might do something special."

"Yeah?" I tired not to get too excited.

"I decided I'll take my top off and you can look at me with nothing on," she said, "only that's all. For tonight, anyway."

"Okay," I said. Laurie likes to do everything by slow stages. We didn't even get around to kissing on the lips till a couple of months after we went out.

She stood up and stepped about six feet away from me. Then she took her T-shirt off. She stood there with her hands at her sides looking really embarrassed.

"Can I use binoculars?" I said.

All I meant was she was so far away, but she turned

red. "You mean they're so small you can't see them otherwise?"

"No, Laurie, they're beautiful. I can see them. I just thought you might come a little closer."

"Will you promise not to touch?"

"Sure."

She moved a few feet closer. I sat there, gazing at them in a trance. It wasn't until about three minutes later that Laurie glanced over to the door and let out a scream. Ranger was standing there, staring at both of us. "Breasts," he said, pointing.

We hadn't locked the door because we assumed he was asleep. When Laurie let out the scream, Ranger started to howl. I got panicked for fear her parents would wake up. I closed the door and shoved him quickly into the room. "Hey, Laurie, don't cry," I said. "it's okay."

"I got so scared!" she said. She had pulled her T-shirt back on. Then she looked at Ranger who was snuffling in the corner. "What's *wrong* with you? Why did you come in here?"

"I had a bad dream." He looked like he was about to cry again.

Laurie clung to me. "He's going to tell Mom and Daddy! They won't let me ever see you again! I can't stand it!"

I kept stroking and patting her. "I'll take care of it," I said. "I'll put him back to bed. . . . Come on, Ranger."

"I want Laurie to come too," he said stubbornly. He had on these droopy pajamas with feet that kids that age always wear.

"Laurie's not feeling well. Come on, I know a good cure for bad dreams that I'll tell you about."

He looked at me suspiciously.

I held out my hand. "Come on. It works for me. It's foolproof."

We went into his room. His bed was kind of smelly, but I couldn't tell if it was wet or just smelly from other nights. I tucked him in. "What you do is this. You try and remember all the bad guys in your dream and you line them all up in your mind and then you give them a good talking to. You tell them they're just dumb, stupid monsters who aren't really scary at all."

"But they are scary," Ranger said.

"They don't know you're scared. If you make fun of them enough, they start to think, maybe they're not scary and they go away. They find some other little kid to bother." I was basically making this up as I went along. Ranger was beginning to look sleepier.

"Laurie has breasts," he said, putting his thumb in his mouth.

"Right, only you won't tell your mom and daddy about that because they might not want you waking her up in the middle of the night."

"Okay." He nodded sleepily. "Do *you* have breasts?"

"No." I raised my T-shirt to show him. "I'm a boy, like you."

"Laurie's a boy," Ranger said.

"No, Laurie's a girl. That's how come she's your sister."

"She's my sister?" Ranger repeated and right in the middle of that sentence he fell asleep.

When I went back to Laurie's room, she was in her nightgown. "I made him promise not to tell."

Laurie hugged me. "Why did I scream? What if they had heard?"

"They didn't."

"He *always* does that! He walks so quietly, you don't even *hear* him! . . . What right does he have to see my breasts? He's my brother and anyway, he's just six years old!"

I kissed her. "I'm glad *I* saw them."

"I'm so dumb and neurotic," she said, leaning against me. "How can you like me?"

"I love you," I said, holding her close. I could feel her breasts through the nightgown. Having seen them made them more real.

"I love you, too."

It wasn't until I was going down in the elevator that I realized it was the first time Laurie and I ever said that to each other. I know you're supposed to think it over first, but it just came out. It doesn't mean we're engaged to be married or anything like that. I felt good going home, like the whole earlier part of the evening had vanished—Dad and the restaurant and *amor fati*. I think I handled the situation with Ranger really well. Maybe I should be a child psychologist when I grow up. But the best part without any question was the moment Laurie took her T-shirt off and stood there, so awkwardly, looking straight ahead. I guess I'm the first boy who's ever seen her breasts. That's kind of an honor. And I meant what I said earlier, even before I saw them. So what if they were five times as big? They wouldn't necessarily be five times nicer. I think they're perfect just the way they are.

When I got home, it was past midnight, so I had to use the downstairs key. Usually there's a night doorman on duty, but sometimes he goes down to the basement to have a sandwich or check on the boiler. If you stood there waiting for him to come up, it could take twenty minutes, and you could get mugged ten times over.

Mom was sitting up in the dining room, working at her desk. It was past midnight, but she usually doesn't wait up, especially for me, to see if I'm home. "Did you have a nice evening?" she asked.

I'd almost forgotten about the part with Dad in the restaurant. "Yeah, it was great."

"Where did you go after you ate? To a show?"

"No, I just went to Laurie's house. . . . I guess Gary took Alexandra home." I'm lucky not to be dating someone who lives in Brooklyn.

Mom got up from her desk and stretched. "Harold turned in early. He felt bushed. . . . Want a snack, hon?"

"Sure, why not?" I got a glass of chocolate milk and a brownie.

"You know, Evan, I've been thinking," Mom said. "Are you sure it's okay with Laurie's parents that you're seeing each other so much?"

"It's not so much," I said.

"What I mean is, you're both so young to have an exclusive relationship. You're just fourteen!"

As though I don't know how old I am! "It's not an exclusive relationship," I explained. "We can both see anyone else we feel like."

"But you don't seem to. Remember how last year the phone was always ringing and you saw someone different almost every week?"

"Yeah, but they were more friends who happened to be girls," I explained. "They weren't *girlfriends*."

"Gary didn't even go out on his first date till he was sixteen," Mom said.

"So? He's socially retarded! Do I have to be too?" That really got me pissed. She should be glad she has at least one normal son.

Mom was looking uncomfortable. "Maybe I'm not putting this right. What I mean is, girls are really vulnerable, at all ages. And I get the feeling Laurie really likes you. I just don't want you to take advantage of that, just out of, well, curiosity or whatever."

It's amazing with mothers the kind of extrasensory perception they have about things. Did she know about my having seen Laurie's breasts for the first time? "It's not curiosity," I said. "If you like someone, you . . . I don't know."

Mom looked at me keenly. "You what?"

Boy, did I not want to go any further in this conversation. I'm not in the habit of lying to Mom, but I didn't feel like telling her the truth. "You want to express it, kind of."

There was a long silence while I waited for Mom to ask, "How?" But she didn't. Instead she said, "Ev, I don't mean to pry into your personal life. I hated it when my mother did that. I know you're a responsible kid. It's just that I'm fond of Laurie."

I grinned. "Me, too." I'm fond of all of her, even the parts I haven't seen yet.

Mom laughed. "Okay, discussion closed."

"Don't worry. I'll let you know when you're about to become a grandmother."

"Evan!"

She figured I was joking. I suppose I was. Laurie thinks you should practically be engaged before anything really serious goes on. Mom really doesn't have that much to worry about, unfortunately.

11

FOR THE NEXT COUPLE OF WEEKS KARIM AND I met at his apartment to go over the routines we were planning for our debut as cheerleaders. We'd decided that our first appearance would be at the Haines-City and Country game in May. They hold the girls' softball games in Central Park. They spectators sit on the grass along the sides.

We'd worked out three basic cheers. They aren't that original, but I figure just our doing it is original enough. One goes:

Give me an **H**
Give me an **A**
Give me an **I**
Give me an **N**
Give me an **E**
Give me an **S**

We love Haines!
INXS

I hope it's okay that we're referring to an actual existing rock group, but part of the idea is we're going to look like rock stars and we wanted a reference the girls would recognize. Even if most of them haven't actually seen INXS in concert, I imagine they've heard of them. The other cheer is:

Haines girls pitch
Haines girls sing.
Haines girls can do any-
thing!

And the final one is:

Our team is fast
And also quick.
There ain't no one
We can't lick.

Haines!
Haines!
Yay!

Harold told us a little about the cheers they used to do at his college, Yale. When he went there, it was all men, so the cheerleaders were men too. It's funny when you think about it. Men have cheered for men's teams, and women have cheered for men's teams. But no one seems to want to cheer for women's teams, even women. It doesn't make that much sense.

"Many things about the world don't make that much sense," Harold said. "Most people do things because they've always been done a certain way. Then one day someone says, 'Hey, this way is dumb. Why don't we change?' And they do. But it can take centuries!"

I thought of what Mr. Shahbaz had said about being innovators. "Like in business, right?" I said. "That's how people get really rich, by being smarter than anybody else."

"No, I don't know about that," Harold said. "I'm smart, but I'm not rich. Not everyone *wants* to be rich, Ev, believe it or not."

"Really? You mean they'd rather be poor?"

"No, but wealth, per se, isn't that important to everyone. What can you do with money?"

"Buy things?" I suggested. I don't think *I'd* have any trouble figuring out what to do about money, if I every had any.

"Right, so you have a lot of things? Then what? It's all pretty limited."

I guess I look at that differently than Harold does. Like say, I was rich enough to buy an airplane, I could learn to fly and just fly anywhere around the world I felt like! And if I were really rich, I wouldn't have to go to work every day like most people. I could sleep late or take Laurie to a show or eat at the House of Chan every day. It doesn't sound limited to me.

Susie finally finished our cheerleading outfits the week before the game with City and Country. They were neat. She said she tried different kinds of fabrics, but the one she chose for the jeans was this crinkly kind of black stuff that glimmered. But the best were the shirts. They buttoned down the front and were made of a silvery material that had little stars woven in. Every time you moved, the stars caught the light. There were leather jackets to wear over the shirts too. "Once you start moving around and getting hot, you just take the jackets off," Susie said. "How does yours feel, Evan? Is it too tight?"

Normally I wouldn't wear things this tight, but I remembered how Rachel said she thought the point of cheerleading was to get the guys excited so they'd want to win. So why shouldn't we get the girls excited too? "No, it's fine," I said.

We ran through our cheers for her. In the first one, I have my drum around my neck and while Karim is doing his jumps, I give him the beat. Karim isn't bad. It took him a long time to get into it, but now he really unwinds and gets going.

Susie whistled. "You're going to knock 'em dead."

"Do you think it will help them win?" Karim asked.

"Sure it will," Susie said. "That's what the guys told us. It means a lot, a whole lot."

From what Laurie has said, the Haines softball team has a slightly uneven record. So far they've lost three games and won two. Laurie's the catcher, but she says she's a pretty good hitter, also.

"Are you nervous?" she asked me the night before on the phone.

"No, what's there to be nervous about?"

"Well, I heard some of the guys are coming just hoping you'll make fools of yourselves."

"That's their problem."

"I don't get why you wouldn't let me and Arlene see your cheers ahead of time."

"It's going to be a surprise," I said. "It's more fun that way."

I guess also, deep down, I wasn't sure they would necessarily like our costumes or the cheers, but I felt it was too late to back out now. I didn't know about other guys from our class coming, hoping we'd be terrible. I'd figured it would be just girls. What if the guys boo when we come out? But I don't think they'd do that, since it's our school. They've got to have some school spirit.

It was a perfect day for a softball game. Hot, but with a cool breeze. In the morning it was overcast, but by three, when school let out, the sun was shining. We all walked over to Central Park, which is only about a quarter of a mile from the school. Karim and I had decided to change into our outfits right after the fourth inning. There's a men's room not too far from the playing field. We had our stuff, except for my drum, in a canvas bag.

They had a pretty good turnout, not as many as for the boys' softball games by any means, but Laurie said it was around twice as many as usually showed up. I saw Ms. Boorstein in the front row. The guys in our class didn't show up at all, not that they usually would, but I'd heard they were boycotting it because they thought it was such a stupid idea. I have to admit that the first four innings were pretty slow. Haines's first pitcher, Dara Cohen, was a real disaster. Laurie claimed later she'd just gotten over a bad virus. She pitched so slow it was like watching a slow-motion movie. Fortunately the other team wasn't amazingly quick either. One girl got a triple, but she never made it to home base. Laurie did okay. She was walked the first time she came up to bat, and tried to bunt a single, but they tagged her. By the end of the third inning the score was 1-0, in favor of City and Country.

Karim and I walked off, trying to look inconspicuous. Once we were out of sight of the game, we started jogging. We changed in a couple of seconds, and then walked back more slowly. We didn't want to get out of breath before we even started. We got back just as the fourth inning was over. Then we ran onto the field and did our cheers.

It's not often that you have the undivided attention of so many people. In one way it's scary, because every little thing you do is being noticed. On the other hand, it's a real turn-on. You want to do your best in a way you don't feel at all when you're just rehearsing. I guess I have a ham streak that I didn't know about before. Anyway, I never felt it when I acted in plays at school. In a play you stand there in some uncomfortable costume that your mother made and you know you're not Captain Hook or the Ghost of Christmas Past or whatever you're supposed to be. I've always wondered that about actors. How can they get into it if they know it's all fake?

The good thing about this was it was *half* real. We weren't pretending to be anyone other than who we really were. But with those outfits on we did look a lot sexier and more dramatic than the way we normally do. Even Karim did, and I'm basically sexier than he is, I think. What also helped was once we'd gotten through one of the cheers, the audience started screaming and cheering along with us. Some of the girls jumped up and down, just like in a rock concert.

When we walked off the field, about thirty girls charged over and started trying to talk to us. Some of them wanted our autographs.

"Could you say, 'To Jane, much love, Evan'?" asked some girl I didn't even know.

I just signed it, "To Jane. Good luck!" I didn't want to get into any kind of trouble, especially with Laurie right there.

"Are you a real singer?" another girl asked. "Do you have an album?"

"No, we're just eighth-grade students," I said.

"What country are you from?"

"Karim's from Saudi Arabia. I'm from Eighty-third and Columbus."

"Would you do it for *our* team?" The girl who asked that was really pretty, with long shimmery blond hair. "We don't have any cheerleaders."

I smiled. "Sorry. We represent Haines and no one else."

She smiled back. "Hey, have you ever been on TV? You look like that boy in the McDonald's commercial."

At that point Ms. Sherman, the coach, came striding over. "Girls, we are in the middle of a softball game! Could you please return at once to your seats? There will be no intercourse with the cheerleading section until the game is over! Is that clear?"

Obviously she meant *intercourse* in a general sense, but one girl said, "We just wanted to *talk* to them."

Karim and I sat down under a tree. He rolled his eyes. "Three girls gave me their phone numbers," he whispered.

"Any cute ones?"

"I can't remember. Some were from the other school."

I lowered my voice. "One of them asked if we'd cheer for their school."

"Of course not! The whole point is to make Haines win." He looked embarrassed. "But we could still go out with them even if they go to the other school, couldn't we?"

"Sure, it's a free country." Then I thought of Laurie. "At least *you* can."

"Laurie wouldn't like it if you did?"

"Well, there's no law that says I can't." I remembered what Mom had said about how I was too young for an exclusive relationship.

Karim smiled. "One of them asked, 'Are you related to Mick Jagger?'"

"One of them thought I was on TV!"

For the rest of the game we sat there basking in the memory of how successful we had been.

DESPITE OUR GREAT CHEERLEADING, HAINES lost 6-5. Still, in the last bunch of innings they did, if not catch on fire, get going to some extent. Laurie hit a double, which enabled her friend Arlene to get to home base. If there'd been one more person on base, they could have evened it up. Still, maybe if it wasn't for us, they wouldn't even have done that well. Laurie had told me that City and Country had one of the better girls' softball teams in the metropolitan area. I have to admit that as a sports event it wasn't one of the more exciting ones I've ever seen. I won't tell Laurie that, though.

She came over and hugged me. "You were great!" she said. "Everyone loved you!"

Just then another surge of girls came over, around

twice as many as the first time, pawing at us, wanting more autographs.

"Do you have a girlfriend?" one of them asked.

"Yes!" Laurie yelled. "Me! And my father's in the Mafia, so anyone who goes after him dies! Got it?"

"I was just asking," the girl said, slinking off.

"Did you make up your own cheers?" another one asked, pushing forward.

"Yeah." I was trying to sign a slip of paper for someone else. In the background were cries of "Let me borrow your pen!" and "Move away, you already talked to him!"

A tall girl in glasses asked if she could interview me quickly for her school paper. I said she could if it was only a couple of questions.

She took out a pad and pencil. "Why did you and your friend decide to be cheerleaders?"

"Well, one of our teachers explained how it wasn't fair that the girls didn't have anyone to cheer for their teams, so we decided to give it a try."

"Did you realize you were going against tradition?" the girl asked. "There aren't cheerleaders for any girls' teams in any New York schools.

"Yeah, that's why we did it," I said. "We wanted to, like, set a precedent."

"Do you think now that you've broken the ice, as it were, more boys will join you?"

I hadn't really thought about that. I looked over at the crowd which was breaking up. There were some boys there, but none of them seemed to want our autographs. "I don't know," I said.

She smiled. "Well, thanks, and good luck!"

Two girls had been standing off to one side as the newspaper reporter interviewed me. They looked about nine or ten years old. After the reporter walked away, they just stood there, staring at me and gigling. "Can I help you?" I asked.

They just kept giggling. Finally one of them said, "Do you have a . . . a girl—" She couldn't get the rest of the words out so her friend said, "Do you like girls?"

I grinned. "Sure."

Laurie marched over with her arms crossed. "Scram!" she said. "He's mine. Got it?"

Somehow the way she said "He's mine" got me mad. "Slavery's dead," I said coolly.

"What do you mean?"

"I mean, I'm not yours or anyone else's. I don't *belong* to anyone."

Laurie flushed. "Well, *you* certainly got a swelled head in record time." Most of the girls were dispersing, but she yelled out, "Here he is—he's going free to anyone who'll butter him up enough!" And with that she marched off.

Karim came over to my side. "How many phone numbers did you get?" he said.

I had stuffed all the scraps of paper in my pocket. "I don't know," I said gloomily. Boy, Laurie sure has a rotten temper.

Karim and I walked to the bus stop. "We were a great success," he said.

"Yeah."

"So why do you look so gloomy?"

"I don't know."

I didn't really feel like talking about it.

The next day at school was a madhouse. For one thing, guys kept coming up to me all day from all the grades, mostly fourth through ninth, saying they wanted to join the cheerleading team too.

"Where do we sign up?" one little guy asked. He wasn't much taller than Ranger.

"Yeah, we want to join," his friend said. "We'd be good. We're strong.

Willy, from our class, took us aside at lunch hour. "At first it sounded like kind of a dumb idea, but why shouldn't the girls have someone on their side? I'll help out if you need me."

That really got me—his pretending that without him the whole project would go under. As my father always says, "Where are these guys when you need them?"

"We want to do it for the girls' tennis team," one boy said. "Do they have a cheerleading section yet?"

I knew that was because the prettiest girl in school, Edanna Carroll, was on the tennis team. The other thing that got me pissed was *we* had done it for the cause of women's rights and to be innovators. These guys just thought it was a way to get girls after you. The ones who came to the game must have reported back, and word had spread.

Marlon handed me a scrap of paper, "Can I have your autograph, Evvie Wevvie? I'm going to put it over my bed and stare at it all night."

"Bug off," I said.

After school Karim went with me to the Bagel Shop.

"My mother is out of her mind," he said. "She thinks it's all because she made such wonderful outfits for us."

"They *were* wonderful," I said, "but what do we do now? We can't have her make them for fifty other guys."

"Why not?" Karim said. "She can have them run up at her factory."

I bit into my bagel. It was toasted and spread with tons of butter, the way I like it. "Yeah, but the thing is, do we *want* all these guys horning in on our idea?"

"We can't cover *all* the girls' teams," Karim said. "We led the way; now it's an open field."

"It's still our idea," I said. "We should at least coordinate and organize it."

"How?"

"Well, I think we should have a meeting at school of all the guys who want to cheerlead for the girls' teams. We can appoint leaders for all the groups, but they have to report back to us."

Karim looked worried. "That's a big responsibility."

"We can do it."

"You're always so self-confident," Karim said admiringly. "I want to be like that someday."

I sighed. "I'm not, really. Basically, I just act that way, and most people are taken in. Sometimes I think I'm just a jerk."

Karim laughed. "You're the hero of the whole school!"

"You, too! Without you, it never would have gotten off the ground."

Laurie still wasn't talking to me, but I had too much pride to admit to anyone, even Karim, that that bothered me. That night I got around ten phone calls from girls

I didn't even know, asking a lot of personal things. I talked to most of them a little, just to get an idea of their personalities. I figured if any of them sounded excellent, I might give them a try. Laurie may *think* she owns me, but she doesn't! The tenth time the phone rang, Harold started to laugh. "This is unbelievable. . . . No, don't get it, Ev. I think it's for me this time." A minute later he came back and points to me. "What can I say?"

The voice on the phone sounded very young, second or third grade, maybe. Sometimes girls' voices are deceptive, they can sound older than they are, but this one wasn't. "Um . . . are you Evan Siegal?"

"Yeah?"

"My name is Sally and my friend's name is Bethe, Bethe with an *e*, but you don't pronounce the *e*, okay? So, the reason why we're calling is we wondered if you'd mind if we started a fan club about you?"

"A fan club?"

"See, you wouldn't have to do anything, just send us a photo if you have one. . . . *Do* you have one?"

"But what's the fan club for?"

"Just, you know, like a club, to talk about you and stuff. Do you mind?"

"I guess not."

"Okay, well, here's my address." And she gave me an address somewhere on East Eightieth Street.

When I got back to the table, Mom was serving dessert. "Hey, Mom, I wasn't finished."

"Well, I'm sorry, Evan. We can't all sit around waiting for you to field all these phone calls."

I dug into the chocolate éclair. "Maybe I should get an unlisted number.

'Gimme a break," Gary said. For someone who scored almost 800 on the verbal part of the SATs, he certainly has a limited range of expressions.

"Well, what am I supposed to do? Just because they want to start an Evan Siegal Fan Club. Can I tell them no and break their hearts? These are little kids!"

"They're not all so little," Gary said. "There's a girl in our class who was talking about you too."

"Who?" I said eagerly.

"It doesn't matter. She's seventeen."

"I really think fan clubs are going *much* too far," Mom said. "It doesn't make any sense." She poured some coffee for Harold.

"I don't know," Harold said. "I've never stopped anyone from forming a Harold Bishop Fan Club. It's just that no one has ever asked."

"All you did was get up and do a bunch of cheers," Gary said. "What's the big deal? Why're they getting all excited."

I shrugged.

"Lemmings," Harold said. "People are like lemmings. One person runs to the sea, and everyone runs. Next year it'll be a new fad."

"It's *not* a fad," I said angrily. "If anything, it's just a beginning."

Mom looked at me. "Laurie must be really proud," she said.

I didn't say anything.

"I would be if *my* boyfriend formed a cheering section," Mom went on.

At that, Harold leaped to his feet and started jumping in the air, yelling, "Holly! Holly, we love you! *H* is for happiness, *O* is for oil, double L spells loveliness, *Y* is—What can I do for Y? Quick, someone, help me."

Mom grabbed him and began kissing him. "Thou dope!"

Gary glanced at me. I guess, even though we're both glad Mom and Harold are happy together, it can be embarrassing when they show it too much.

I went to my room to finish my math homework. It was a letdown that, despite all this adulation, I still had homework, Laurie was still mad at me, I still had to get to school at 8:30 A.M. and make my bed and start supper on Monday and Friday when Mom got home late. You'd think I could get special privileges of some kind. I decided to write to Dad about being a cheerleader. I like writing him things that'll cheer him up and make him proud of me.

Dear Dad:

That was an excellent meal at the House of Chan. Laurie said to thank you. She said it was the best Chinese meal she ever ate.

Basically, nothing is new . . . except for one thing. I told you how Karim and I decided to be cheerleaders for the girls' softball team? Well, many kids at school made fun of us and thought it was dumb. Then we did it. You can't believe what a success we were! I'm not saying that just to boast. I had to sign hundreds of autographs and some girls started an Evan Siegal Fan club.

Mom is afraid it will give me a swelled head, but it won't. I just think it was a smart idea.

Hope your business is going well.

Love,
Evan

Actually, I couldn't remember if I had told him we were going to do it, but I know I did mention about Karim being my friend, I probably shouldn't have said "hundreds" of autographs. Dozens would have been more accurate. But our English teacher, Mr. Blair, says you can exaggerate if it helps amplify your point.

13

THE NEXT WEEK KARIM AND I PUT A SIGN UP on the school bulletin board saying there was going to be a meeting of any guys who wanted to cheerlead for the girls' teams. We asked permission, like you're supposed to, to hold it in the rec room, which is on the ground floor. About thirty guys showed up. Most of them were little guys, fourth to seventh grade, but there were about a dozen from the high school.

"The thing is, Kar and I can't organize every group," I said, "so we're going to appoint leaders for each girls' team, and then you can meet with your leader and he'll report back to us. Now, how many want to do it for softball?"

About half of them raised their hands.

Karim looked at me. "Too many."

I tried to talk loud so they all could hear me. "Guys,

this is too many for just one cheerleading section. How about the tennis team? Or the basketball team? Volleyball? Soccer?"

"Basketball's over for this season," someone said.

"Yeah, but we're not talking about just this one season. We've got to start planning ahead for next year," I said. "Basketball is just as important as softball, and the games are held in the gym, so probably there's more of an audience." Actually I don't know if there's any audience, but maybe this will bring more guys out just to watch.

"I think five or six per group is the best," Karim said.

"What do you know?" some little guy called out.

Karim turned red. "I am the organizer of the cheerleading team. Evan and I started it."

"*He* started it," the boy said. He was short and chubby with curly black hair. "Not you."

"We started it together," I said. "Karim's mother made the outfits. He was in on it from the beginning, unlike some." I noticed Willy in the group.

"How can he know about cheerleading if he isn't American?" the boy persisted.

"He knew just as much about it as I did," I said. "Which was nothing, basically. We just made up an act and did it."

"I thought you were supposed to be experts," another boy said.

"Now we are," I said, "but we weren't in the beginning. Now we know a lot about it."

It wasn't as easy getting the whole thing worked out as I'd thought. Despite what we said, most of them still wanted to be on the softball cheerleading section. We took down six names and the rest we foisted off on the other sports. We decided to appoint mainly eighth graders, like us, to lead the groups. Some of these little kids didn't even know what they were signing up for. They'd just heard about it, and to them it sounded like fun. You could tell they might not even take it seriously.

"Hey, listen, you guys, this is a lot of work," I said. "I hope you realize that. You have to practice, and you have to yell real loud so everyone can hear you. That's not easy if you're out-of-doors. And you have to be in good shape physically."

The chubby little boy eyed me nervously. "How good?"

Karim said he'd take the lists home and make photocopies. By the time the meeting was over, it was four o'clock. School had let out over an hour earlier. There wasn't a whole gang of kids waiting outside the way there usually is. Just as I was walking out, Rachel stepped out of the principal's office. "Hi," I said. "How come you're here so late?"

"I answer the phone for the PTA today," she said. "How'd the meeting go?"

"It was pretty good. . . . It may be a lot of work, though."

She started walking alongside me down the street. Her hair was in a ponytail that swung back and forth, and she smelled good. "You know, Evan, I really feel like I ought to apologize to you."

"What for?"

"Well, when you brought the idea up about the cheerleading thing, it just seemed . . . strange. And maybe I was jealous because I've always been a cheerleader and I thought, oh, no, here the guys are horning in, even on that."

"We only did it because you said you wouldn't volunteer for the girls' team."

"I know! But anyhow, what I meant to say is I think it was a super idea! Why *shouldn't* girls have cheerleaders for their teams too? In fact, I was thinking maybe we should sort of, you know, coordinate the cheerleading teams, have boy *and* girl cheerleaders for all the sports."

I was silent. "You mean, for the boys' teams, too?"

"Yeah, we could all meet and maybe alternate the cheering? Or even have some cheers with boys and girls together." She looked at me eagerly.

"I don't know," I said slowly. "I never thought of that."

"Why don't you come over to my house for dinner, and we can talk about it some more?"

I looked at my watch. "I'd have to call my mother."

We were just passing a phone booth. "Okay, call!" Rachel said. "I'll wait."

Mom said it was okay as long as I came back in time to do my homework. Rachel lives just about ten blocks from me so I didn't think it would be a problem. I was at her house once before when she gave a big birthday party in seventh grade. "Is it okay with your mother?" I asked.

"Oh, sure. You don't have any special food fetishes, do you?"

"No, I can eat anything."

"Good, because there's no telling what it'll be. Nothing fancy, though."

Even though there was nothing wrong with what I was doing, I was glad school had cleared out and no one saw me walking off with Rachel. It's annoying. She can really get me mad a lot of times by the way she acts, but I still felt proud and, I have to admit, even a little excited going to her house alone. I tried to keep my eyes fastened on her face, but even if you don't look at her figure, you know it's there. Maybe she'll feel like showing me her breasts too, now that I'm such a big deal around the eighth grade.

Rachel's mother was in the kitchen, fixing supper. "Hi, Evan," she said. She was a lot younger looking and prettier than Laurie's mother. "We've been hearing a lot about you lately."

I turned red. "It's nice to meet you."

It turns out Rachel's family eats early, on the nose of six, and Rachel had to set the table, so we didn't even go into her room. Her father was lying down, but when Rachel yelled "Supper!" he came ambling out of the bedroom.

Just as we were sitting down at the table, a little girl who looked about ten years old came in. She looked like a small, skinny version of Rachel. Rachel smiled. "Bethe, this is Evan Siegal."

I've read that expression *struck dumb* lots of times, but I can't remember ever seeing anyone *actually* struck dumb. Bethe just stopped dead in her tracks and stared at me with her mouth open. I looked back at her and smiled. When she finally got her voice back, she said very quietly, "I may faint."

Rachel said, "Bethe and her friend Sally have formed an Evan Siegal fan club."

I remembered their names from that phone call. "Hi, Bethe."

Bethe slid into her chair, keeping her eyes fixed on me the whole time. "Boy, I can't believe it," she said. "I can't believe this is really happening."

"I told you he was my friend," Rachel said.

Rachel's mother passed around meat loaf and corn. "How does it feel to be a celebrity, Evan?"

"Well, I don't exactly understand it," I said. "I mean, I wanted it to be successful, but I don't get why just getting up and doing a few cheers gets these girls so excited."

"Yeah, it's true," Rachel said. "No one ever formed a fan club for us."

All the time I ate, I could see Bethe's eyes focused just on me, like if she looked away one second, I might disappear. It was a little unnerving.

"Quit staring at him!" Rachel said. "You'll make him self-conscious."

"I just can't believe it," Bethe said. "You're right here in our house!"

"Listen, I've known him since kindergarten," Rachel said. "He's just a regular person, not a god, so cool it."

"Mom," Bethe said, "can I invite Sally over after dinner? She'd kill me if she knew Evan was here and I'd hogged him all to myself."

Rachel's mother smiled. "You're not going to invite the whole club over, are you?"

"No," Bethe said.

"Mom, Evan and I have stuff to talk about," Rachel said. "We need some privacy."

"My mom wants me home not too late," I said. "I have some math homework to do."

"You can do that here," Rachel said. "I did it while I was in the principal's office. It's not too hard."

Bethe ran to the phone.

Rachel signed. "Only, Mom, seriously, I don't want the whole evening to be Bethe and Sally standing around gawking at Evan. We really do have something to discuss."

"I won't let them gawk," her mother said.

What was strange was her father just sat there reading a book during the whole meal. He never said anything. As we went into Rachel's room, I asked, "Does your father always read while he eats?" Mom won't let us do that, ever. She says it's rude.

"Yeah, he's kind of antisocial," Rachel said, "but he's not so bad otherwise. I used to be ashamed to have my friends meet him."

I thought of my father. "I know what you mean."

"It usually turns out their fathers are just *as* weird," she said, "*or* their mothers, or both. I can't think of anyone I know who has two normal parents like you see on TV."

I thought of Laurie's parents. They seem pretty normal. "Yeah, I know what you mean."

Rachel's room was big and one whole wall was covered with magazine rip-outs of various rock groups, mostly Duran Duran. My mother would kill me if I did that. I sat down next to her on the bed. Rachel smiled at me. "Boy, I've had a lot of fantasies about this situation," she said.

"What kind?" My heart started thumping.

"I'm not going to tell you. You might think I have a dirty mind." She looked at me sideways again. "I think I just have a lively imagination."

What was bothering me was not only the thought of Laurie, but the thought of Karim and how much he liked Rachel. "Do you like Karim?" I said. "He did the cheerleading too."

"He was just copying you," Rachel said contemptuously. "He just copies everything you do. He isn't original like you are."

"Actually, he was the one who thought of most of the cheers," I said.

"But you had the *idea*," Rachel said. "He would never have gotten up in class and volunteered when everyone was making fun of it." She gazed at me admiringly. "Listen, I know he's your friend and all. It's just that you can't force yourself to like someone if you don't."

"True," I said. We were sitting so close I was beginning to feel really attracted to her.

"That night we went over to his house," Rachel said, "and I began kissing him, the only way I could get through it was to close my eyes and pretend he was you."

I sighed. "There's also Laurie."

"I heard you broke up with her."

"Well, we had a fight, but—"

Just then the door opened. It was Bethe and her friend Sally. Sally was a little taller with blond hair that hung in her face, and braces. She had a Polaroid camera around her neck. "It's really true!" she said.

"Do you think I'd make it up?" Bethe said.

"Bethe, you're supposed to knock before you come in," Rachel said irritably.

"Well, pardon me if we were interrupting something," Bethe said. She and Sally giggled.

Then Sally stepped forward. "Can I take your picture, Evan? My father lent me his camera."

"Sure, why not?"

She moved in close. "I'm not sure about how to work this. I never did it before."

Bethe hovered near her. "You focus here. Then you just press down."

Sally took one picture of me, but it was out of focus so she took another. Then they wanted one of the two of them with me, so Rachel took that. "Do you want us to take one of you two together?" Bethe asked.

"Okay," Rachel said. She sat down and put her arm around me.

"You make a really cute couple," Sally said thoughtfully.

"Go on, take it," Bethe said. "They can't sit there like that all night!"

Actually, it wasn't a bad feeling, sitting there with Rachel leaning against me. Maybe I could have sat like that all night.

When they were finished, they both shook hands with me. "Friday the thirteenth," Sally said. "From now on, Friday the thirteenth is going to be my favorite day."

"Me, too," Bethe said.

When they left, Rachel got up and closed the door firmly. "I wish I could have a lock on my door," she said.

"I don't have one on mine either," I said.

I have to admit that after that we did make out a little. She didn't show me her breasts or anything, but it was hard not to be aware of their existence, as it were. As I left, Rachel said, "Maybe Friday the thirteenth will be *my* favorite day from now on too."

14

When I asked Karim how he felt about the idea of a boy-girl combined cheerleading team, he said firmly, "Never."

I was surprised. "Why not?"

"They didn't want to do it in the beginning," he said. "Now they're just trying to cash in on our success."

"Rachel would be part of it," I said. "Doesn't that make any difference?"

"Not to me."

I looked at him in surprise. "How come? I thought you really had a crush on her."

He looked disdainful. "That seems like a hundred years ago," he said. "Arlene says Rachel is an airhead. I agree."

When *I* tried to tell him that a few months ago, it

fell on deaf ears. Arlene! "Since when do you care what Arlene says?"

Karim looked right at me. "Since we started going out."

"You and *Arlene*?"

Karim turned red. "She may not be as good looking, but she's . . . Well, when she takes her glasses off, she's just as good-looking. She has the most beautiful eyes I've ever seen. I'm trying to convince her to get contacts."

I cleared my throat. "Well, that's good," I said diplomatically.

"So, you don't have to worry about me as far as Rachel is concerned," Karim said. "If you want her, that is."

How did he know about me and Rachel? "I just went to her house after school," I said, embarrassed.

"Well, Arlene said Rachel has a photo of the two of you all wrapped up together," Karim said. "She showed it to all the girls . . . including Laurie."

Shit. I should've known Rachel would do something like that. It made me feel lousy.

"So, you and Laurie are washed up?" he said.

I looked at him. "I don't know."

"If you ask me, Laurie's worth a hundred Rachels," Karim said.

"Yeah." I suddenly felt really depressed.

"Look, just call Laurie up and explain it was all a mistake."

"How about the photo?"

"Explain what really happened, that Rachel just forced you to pose and—"

"She didn't force me."

"Ev, you're better at explaining these things than I am. Just invent a convincing story."

I thought of all the convincing stories I'd invented for other people. The trouble is, it's a lot harder if it's someone you care about. "She'll hang up on me," I said. "I *know* it. Laurie has a terrible temper."

"She won't hang up," Karim said.

"You don't know her," I said. "She has a lot of pride, too. She'll never forgive me if she saw that photo."

There was a pause.

"She saw it," Karim said.

"Then forget it. It's all over."

We sat in silence for a couple of minutes. We were in Karim's room. "Would you like me to call for you?" Karim said.

I stared at him. It seemed supremely ironical to have someone call for *me*, the great matchmaker, as Mom sometimes calls me. "Would you?"

"Sure," he said. "After all, she's Arlene's best friend."

"Don't . . . Well, first find out if she wants to get back together," I said. "Don't start in on how I'm pining away or anything."

Karim smiled. "I'll handle it beautifully."

God, to think this guy was having trouble even talking to girls a few months ago! Karim promised to call Laurie that night and to let me know what she'd said before school the next morning.

When I got home, I found a letter from my father. It said:

Dear Evan:

I was delighted to learn of your success as an organizer of the cheerleading team. Someday I have to take lessons from you. You certainly have the winning touch when it comes to the opposite sex.

I have been enjoying the companionship of someone named Harriet. She is divorced and has a daughter your age. So far she seems to like me, but I imagine it's only a matter of time before she discovers my true personality. On the other hand, it may be as I get to know her better, I'll discover she's not for me. But for the moment I feel happy. I hope it's not bad luck to say that in writing.

Good luck and congratulations on your success!

Love,
Julian

A few years ago my father asked me to start calling him Julian. He said otherwise I would always think of him as a father and not as a person. The trouble is, I do think of him as a father, and not as a person, no matter what I call him.

As I lay in bed at night I thought of how ironical it was that, despite being the object of fan clubs and dozens of girls' admiration, despite having the sexiest girls in class like me, I was waiting anxiously for Karim to find out about Laurie. If anyone had told me last year that I'd be in this position, I'd have laughed. And I never would trust anyone except Karim to handle this for me. He's the kind of person you can trust to the grave about anything.

We arranged to meet at the Bagel Shop half an hour

before school started. He was already there. Karim always eats what he considers an American breakfast of eggs with bacon and coffee with milk and sugar. I just have a bagel and a glass of milk. "She's sick," he said.

"With what?"

"A virus. So she couldn't stay on the phone long."

"What'd she say?" I asked anxiously.

"Well, she's kind of upset about the photo."

"Did you tell her I was forced into it?"

Karim looked at his eggs. "She said she didn't see how a boy of fourteen could be physically forced to do something he didn't want to do."

"It wasn't a matter of being physically forced," I said. "I just didn't want to be impolite."

"That's what I said," Karim said.

"What did she say to that?"

"She said she could forgive you if it were anyone but Rachel. She just couldn't understand how anyone she had liked could like anyone who was such a superficial snob."

I set down my bagel. "What'd you say to that?"

"I told her I considered myself a person of excellent taste as well as intelligence, but that even I had had a crush on Rachel for a long time, *without* any encouragement."

"Yeah?" It sounded like he'd done a good job, at least. You have to think fast if you're representing someone who isn't there.

"She said that was excusable because *I* was from another country and it might take me longer to catch on about American girls, but she didn't see what *your* excuse was."

"I thought she was sick." It sounded like a pretty long conversation for someone who was at death's door.

"She was. . . . Anyway, at the end she said she thought you should handle your own affairs and that it was cowardly to have me call up for you."

Boy, talk about things boomeranging! "This was obviously a great idea."

"I told her it wasn't a matter of cowardice, that you didn't want to bother her if she really didn't like you."

I just sat there, looking at him.

"She said, 'Let him find out for himself.'"

I drank my milk. "How am I supposed to find out if she's sick?"

"She'll get better eventually."

These viruses can take a week to ten days when they're serious. I know, because I had one last fall.

At school that day Rachel followed me around like a dog. She seemed to think we had started going together just because I went over to her house one afternoon! I remember how Gary used to say the reason he didn't want to go out with any girl in his class more than a couple of times was they started thinking they were practically engaged to him.

"Do you want some of my lunch?" Rachel said. "My mom makes terrific shrimp-salad sandwiches. We can share."

I do happen to like shrimp salad a lot, and Mom never makes me anything that fancy. In fact, she never makes lunch for me at all now that I'm in eighth grade, so I usually just throw something together in the morning.

"My sister is still so excited about your having come over the other night," Rachel said. "You're practically like a movie star to her. She put that photo right above her bed. I think she may kiss it good night."

I shrugged. "She seemed like a nice person."

"She's okay," Rachel said, "except for her habit of barging into my room without knocking." She smiled at me teasingly.

"Rachel, the thing is, Karim and I were talking about that plan you mentioned, about combining the girl and boy cheerleading sections into one?"

"Yeah?" Rachel smoothed back her hair and looked at me, her lips parted.

"He doesn't think it's a good idea."

"So?"

"What do you mean, so?"

"You're the one who controls everything, Evan. He's just your sidekick."

"He is not," I said indignantly. "He's my friend."

"He'll do anything you say. Just tell him you've decided it's a good idea. He'll fall into line in two seconds."

I set down my shrimp-salad sandwich. "I'm not sure it *is* such a good idea. Boys' cheerleading is different from girls'. We have a different style and approach."

"Oh, come on. What's different about it?"

"It just is. . . . And you're wrong about Karim. This whole thing would never have gotten off the ground if it weren't for him. His mother designed the costumes, he helped me think up the cheers . . ."

Rachel crumpled up the wax paper from her sandwich. "Well, he certainly must be desperate for a girlfriend." She rolled her eyes and looked over toward the other end of the rec room where Karim and Arlene were sitting next to each other, talking.

"He's not desperate," I said. "He's just showing some good sense for a change."

What really got me angry, though, was Rachel's showing that photo of the two of us to everyone, including Laurie. She had to have known the effect that would have. I noticed that while we had lunch together, nobody joined us, which they only do if they assume you're a couple and want privacy. During the last few classes I was pretty preoccupied, but by the end of school I had a plan. I might end up getting a deathly illness, but sometimes you've got to risk it.

15

LAURIE'S PARENTS WORK AND NEVER COME home till six. But when I rang the front doorbell, there was no answer. She could have been sound asleep, but I decided to wait. I rang again, this time really leaning on the doorbell. Finally the seeing-eye thing went up, and I heard a croaky voice say, "Who is it?"

"It's me, Evan."

I got scared for a moment that she might not open the door, but she did. She looked terrible. Her hair was sort of wild looking and her eyes were half shut, her nose all red and crusty. "What are you doing here?" Laurie whispered. "I'm sick. Didn't Karim tell you?"

"He said you thought I should speak for myself and not use him as an intermediary."

Laurie sighed. "I meant on the phone."

"I was afraid you'd hang up."

"I'm covered with germs!" Laurie said. "You'll catch my virus if you come in."

"I'll chance it." I followed her into her room. It had that musty smell rooms get when you're sick. There was a wastebasket stuffed with Kleenexes near her bed.

Laurie collapsed back in bed. "I don't have *any* energy," she said. "I feel like I'm half asleep. My temperature is a hundred and two."

"Do you have the energy to listen to me?"

She nodded.

You know how when people testify in court they're sworn in saying they'll tell "the whole truth and nothing but the truth"? Well I decided to do that. I told everything, how Rachel had come out of the principal's office, how I'd been relieved no one was around, but also a little bit excited. I told about her father's reading at the table and her sister's fan club and her sister's friend coming over with the camera, and Rachel's suggesting the boy-girl cheerleading section. There's only one part I left out—how we made out a little at the end.

"Why were you posing that way in the photo?" Laurie said. Her voice sounded like one of the witches in the school play or like a record playing at the wrong speed, sort of draggy and hoarse.

"She put her arm around me. What could I do?"

"You didn't exactly look like you were struggling that much."

I sighed. "Okay, listen, this is hard to admit. You're going to hate me, but we did make out a little bit too."

"I know," Laurie said limply. "She told us all about it."

"I don't have any excuse," I said. "I'm sorry, though."

Laurie stared at me a long time. "She's gorgeous and she's always been after you. You felt flattered."

"Right," I admitted.

"And you were mad at me for saying, 'He's mine.' I shouldn't have. You're right. Nobody belongs to anybody . . . it's just that I got so hysterical seeing all those girls flinging themselves at you! Fan clubs!"

"Those were just little kids, fourth graders."

"In one second they'll be big," Laurie said. "Wait till next year. They'll go off to summer camp and come back looking like Rachel."

"I think it'll take more than one summer," I said, remembering Bethe and Sally. "Anyhow, I'm not real to them. I'm just a sex symbol."

Laurie laughed. It wasn't as peppy as her usual laugh, but it made her sound more the way she usually does. "Just my luck," she said. "I like a guy, just a regular nice, cute-looking guy, and by the end of the year he's a sex symbol! They'll be putting centerfolds of you up on the wall next."

"Not a chance," I said.

She reached for a Kleenex and blew her nose. "So, what's happening about the boy-girl cheerleading thing?"

"Karim and I decided it was a bad idea. We'll stick to separate but equal."

Laurie smiled. "It's funny. Here, a couple of months ago no one would cheer for us, and now everyone wants to!"

"It's the lemming syndrome," I explained. I told her Harold's theory.

Laurie was sinking back in her pillows again. "Ev, I'm really glad you came over," she said, "but I'm kind of fading again."

"I'll go," I said. "Do you want me to get you some juice or something?"

Laurie held out her glass and asked if I could bring her some orange juice. As I did, Ranger came padding out of his room. He didn't look too hot either. "I'm sick too," he said.

"I'm sorry to hear it."

"Will you pour me some orange juice?"

"Sure."

When I did, he said, "Your system works about dreams, Evan. I've only had two bad ones since then."

"Oh . . . well, good." I carried Laurie's juice back to her room and handed it to her. Then I bent down and kissed her.

"Oh, Ev," she croaked. "You're going to get horribly sick!"

"No," I said. "Your germs are nice, friendly, benign germs."

She laughed her croaky laugh. "At least you've seen me at my absolute and total worst."

"You look beautiful," I told her.

I went home feeling happy.

There were only six more weeks of school after that. Karim and I let four other guys join us for the softball cheerleading section. The others had to work out their own routines, and some of them planned on waiting till fall when the basketball and squash season started. It's funny, though. Once it was a success, it wasn't quite as much fun anymore. That first time, when we went out on the field, just the two of us, not knowing how it would go over was by far the most exciting. We got used to girls coming over for our autographs after each game. It didn't seem to matter if Haines had won or lost. The same number of girls would come over.

The last game of the season was the most exciting Arlene hit a home run in the eighth inning with the bases loaded. Laurie was on second, so she got to score too. It still meant that the overall season record was six losses and five wins, but everyone, including Ms. Sherman, looked extremely pleased. She came over to shake our hands and thank us for what we'd done. "The morale of the team is higher than it's ever been," she said. "You've made the girls feel that what they do is important, win or lose."

"Yeah, well, it is." I looked over at Karim, who had his arm around Arlene. In fact, he was lifting her up in the air. She wears contacts now, but I'd still say she isn't someone you'd pick on the basis of looks alone.

Even Harold and Gary showed up for the final game. Gary came with Alexandra. I saw them sitting under a tree, holding hands. I was sure he'd make some crack, but all he said was, "Good going, Ev. That's some act."

"If I were a girl," Harold said, "I'd join the softball team immediately."

"Did you follow the game?" I asked. Harold always claims he can't understand sports.

"Kind of," Harold said. "It was good when all of

them started running around in a circle and hitting the bases, right?"

"Right." I looked around for Laurie. She was standing next to Arlene and Karim. I waved at her.

She came over and smiled up at me. "Hey, cutie, can I have your autograph?" she said.

Harold laughed. "You can have mine." He took out his camera and took a photo of Laurie and me, she in her softball outfit, me in my cheerleading outfit.

"So, that's how I came to write that article, "I Was a Male Cheerleader," for the Sunday *Daily News*. If you get the *News*, you probably saw it. Mom was afraid the headline was too sensational, but she admitted the article was excellent. I sent photocopies to Dad and all my aunts and uncles. Maybe when I get out of college, I'll be a newspaper reporter. It's true I haven't had a lot of experience yet, but you've got to start somewhere.

About the Author

Norma Klein was born in New York City and graduated cum laude from Barnard College with a degree in Russian. She later received a master's degree in Slavic languages from Columbia University. She began publishing short stories while attending college and has since written novels for readers of all ages. The author gets her ideas from everyday life and advises would-be writers to do the same—to write about their experiences or things they care about.

Seveal of Norma Klein's books are available from Fawcett, including ANGEL FACE, BEGINNER'S LOVE, IT'S OKAY IF YOU DON'T LOVE ME, LOVE IS ONE OF THE CHOICES, THE QUEEN OF WHAT IFS, BIZOU, SNAPSHOTS and GIVE AND TAKE.

Ms. Klein lives in Manhattan with her husband and two teenage daughters.